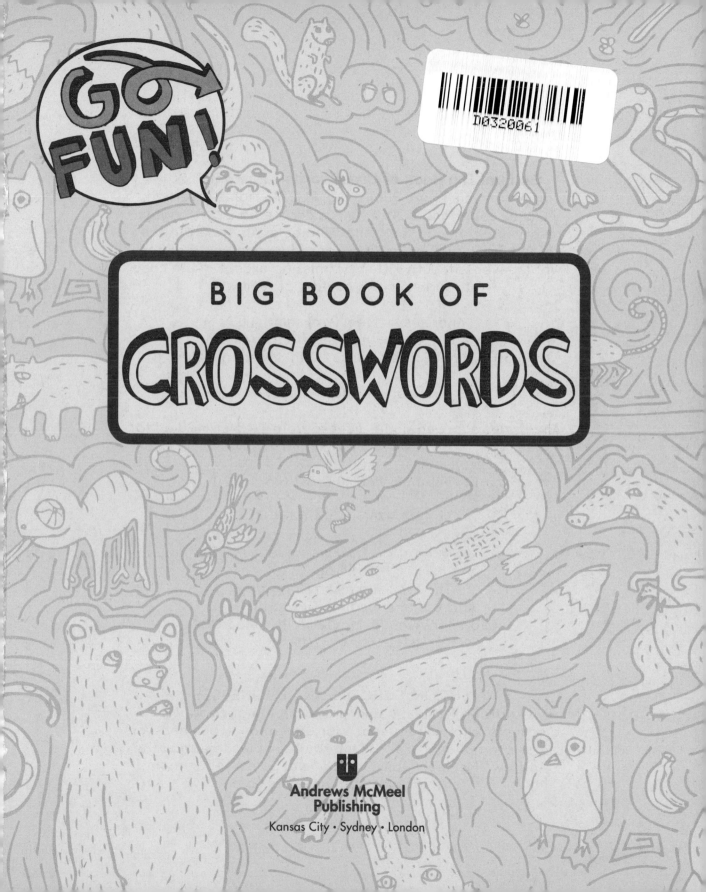

GO FUN!

BIG BOOK OF CROSSWORDS

Andrews McMeel
Publishing

Kansas City • Sydney • London

Andrews McMeel Publishing, LLC
an Andrews McMeel Universal company
1130 Walnut Street, Kansas City, Missouri 64106

www.andrewsmcmeel.com

All puzzles supplied under license from Puzzler Media Ltd.
www.puzzler.com

14 15 16 17 18 PAH 10 9 8 7 6 5 4 3 2 1

ISBN: 978-1-4494-6486-8

Made by:
The P. A. Hutchison Company
Address and location of production:
400 Penn Avenue, Mayfield, PA 18433 USA
1st printing – 7/18/14

1

ACROSS

1 View, look at (3) ✓
2 Pizza ___, restaurant chain (3)
5 Farm vehicle (7) ✓
6 Extend, like elastic (7) ✓
8 Large cup (3) ✓
9 Damp, soggy (3) ✓

DOWN

1 Matching jacket and trousers (4) ✓
3 ___ de France, annual cycle race (4) ✓
4 Fireworks that rise high into the sky (7) ✓
6 Move in the water (4) ✓
7 Command for 'stop marching' (4) ✓

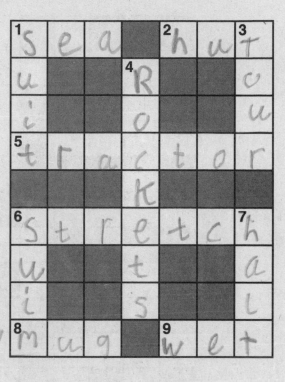

S	E	A		H	U	T
U			R			O
I			O			U
T	R	A	C	T	O	R
			K			
S	T	R	E	T	C	H
W			T			A
I			S			L
M	U	G		W	E	T

2

ACROSS

1 Stain material (3)
3 Crawling insect (3)
5 Pat softly (3)
6 Used a spade (3)
7 Not at home (3)
8 Australian flightless bird (3)
9 I agree (3)
10 Black road-surfacing material

DOWN

1 ___-long-legs, insect (5)
2 Borders (5)
3 Approximately (5)
4 Personal teacher (5)

ugh 4 dady

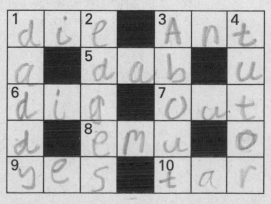

D	I	E		A	N	T
A		D	A	B		U
D	I	G		O	U	T
D		E	M	U		O
Y	E	S		T	A	R

ACROSS

7 England's capital city (6)

8 Oak tree seeds (6)

9 Precious stone (3)

10 ___-hoop, round toy (4)

11 Roald ___, writer (4)

12 Opposite of no (3)

14 Jeans material (5)

17 Elephant's tusk material (5)

19 Stamp or photograph book (5)

20 Summer dish of raw vegetables (5)

22 Black and white bear-like animal (5)

24 Nocturnal bird (3)

26 Edge of a hat (4)

28 Vast, enormous (4)

29 Numbers of years in a decade (3)

30 Flee (6)

31 Response (6)

DOWN

1 Sound level (6)

2 Brainwave (4)

3 Very cross (5)

4 Stays in a tent (5)

5 James ___, 007 (4)

6 Ship's 'brake' (6)

13 Arm joint (5)

15 Zero (3)

16 Crazy (3)

17 Pixie (3)

18 Possess (3)

21 Type of crossword clue (6)

23 Short sword (6)

24 Frequently (5)

25 Of the moon (5)

27 Pork, beef, or ham (4)

28 Snake's noise (4)

4

ACROSS

1 Place to build sandcastles (5)
4 Family of wind instruments (5)
7 Volcanic dust (3)
8 Assist (3)
9 Fishing implement (3)
10 Exam (4)
11 Painter's picture support (5)
14 Sporting occasion (5)
16 One-person act (4)
18 Cooking vessel (3)
20 Get older (3)
21 Move your head to show approval (3)
22 Correct in every detail (5)
23 Segment (5)

DOWN

1 Small pierced ball hung on a necklace (4)
2 Track or field competitor (7)
3 Body's organ for pumping blood (5)
4 Scout or Guide award (5)
5 Layer of gases surrounding the Earth (3)
6 Seat on a horse (6)
12 Total lack of sound (7)
13 Men, women, and children (6)
15 Grilled bread (5)
16 Sharply inclined (5)
17 Outer border (4)
19 Drink made with a bag (3)

5

ACROSS

1 Jump on one leg (3)
3 Animal's foot (3)
5 Light which can be carried (7)
6 Slow-moving creature (5)
9 Person in university education (7)
10 Ocean (3)
11 Knock gently (3)

DOWN

1 Ship's cargo area (4)
2 Piece of land almost surrounded by water (9)
3 Title given to America's leader (9)
4 Part of an airplane (4)
7 Invites (to a party) (4)
8 Rung on a ladder (4)

6

Across And Down

In this mini-crossword, the three answers read the same across and down. See how quickly you can solve it.

1 Fourth month
2 Mechanical helper
3 Ancient language

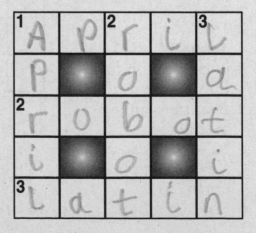

ACROSS
1 Item that resembles a toadstool (8)
6 Space between two things (3)
7 Goods transported by ship (5)
8 Christmas, birthday, or Valentine message (4)
9 'Red' on traffic lights (4)
12 Lower leg joint (5)
14 Put to some purpose (3)
15 Part of a word (8)

DOWN
1 Performer who does tricks (8)
2 Terrific (5)
3 Compete on a track (4)
4 Boat's paddle (3)
5 Finish (8)
10 Part of the hand (5)
11 Ringing instrument (4)
13 Lock opener (3)

8

Word Square

When the answers to the clues are entered into the grid, the words will read the same down and across.

1 Hair on a horse's neck
2 The length times the width
3 Close to
4 Organs of hearing

9

ACROSS

1 Chocolate-flavored milky drink (5)
4 Person who flies an airplane (5)
7 ____ Roy, Scottish hero (3)
8 Pistol or rifle, e.g. (3)
9 Animal's shelter (3)
10 Garden-tidying tool (4)
11 Machine for lifting heavy objects (5)
14 Soap ____, *The Young and the Restless* for example (5)
16 Opposite of 'soft' (4)
18 Become or acquire (3)
20 Long-tailed rodent (3)
21 Honey-making insect (3)
22 Sharp-eyed bird of prey (5)
23 Vacation accommodation (5)

DOWN

1 Christmas, birthday, or Valentine message (4)
2 Green, white, or red leafy vegetable (7)
3 Have a fight, quarrel (5)
4 Contagious fear (5)
5 Removable top for a container (3)
6 Underground route (6)
12 Performer of gymnastic feats, perhaps in a circus (7)
13 Moving part in the mouth (6)
15 Share an opinion (5)
16 Pet rabbit's home (5)
17 Door chime (4)
19 Boat used for guiding ships (3)

Picture This

Write the name of each pictured item into the grid and you will find, reading down the circled letters, the type of fish Rod is about to catch.

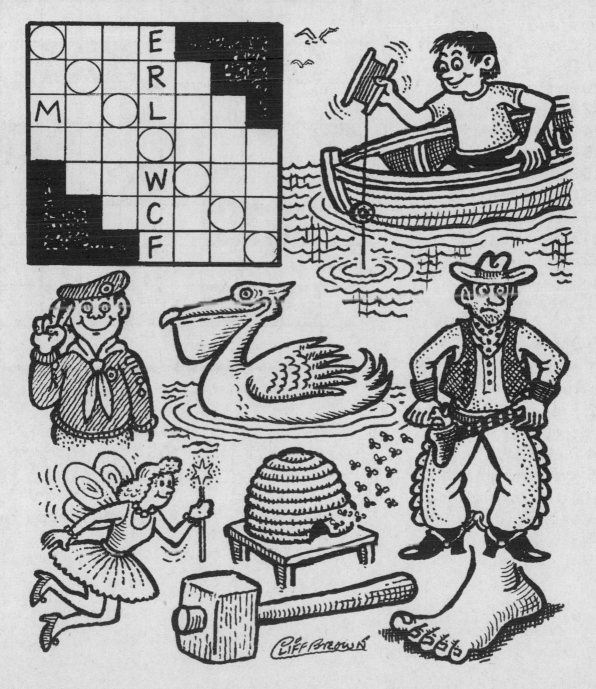

ACROSS

1 Creature with fins (4)
3 Chickens (4)
7 Chopping tool (3)
8 Cow's milk bag (5)
9 Decay (3)
10 Plastic container (3)
12 Male child (3)
14 Coastal bird (7)
15 Tame animal (3)
16 Find the sum (3)
18 Upper limb (3)
19 Not expensive (5)
21 Male adults (3)
22 Plant stalk (4)
23 Round red cheese (4)

DOWN

1 Midnight ___, night-time meal (5)
2 Frozen dessert, like sorbet (7)
4 Finish (3)
5 Warning signal on an emergency vehicle (5)
6 Celebrity's signature (9)
11 Purpose (3)
12 Banged a door shut (7)
13 Not young (3)
15 Discs used in ice hockey (5)
17 Jeans material (5)
20 Female sheep (3)

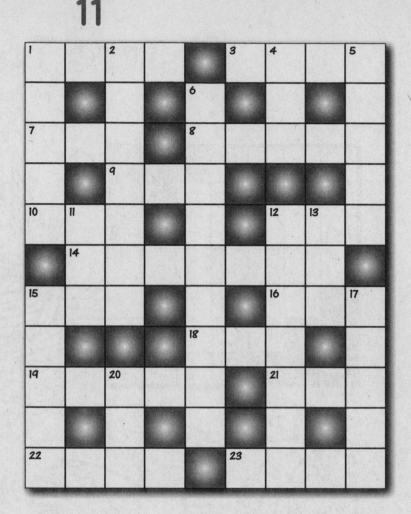

12
Kriss Kross

Fit the listed words in the grid. If you fill in the nine-letter word COMPOSURE that should help you get started. Rearrange the letters in the gray squares to spell out something you might use if you go surfing.

4 letters
ROCK
SLIP
SWAY

5 letters
LURCH
NERVE
POISE
SHAKE
SLIDE

6 letters
STABLE
TREMOR

7 letters
TREMBLE

8 letters
COOLNESS

9 letters
COMPOSURE

10 letters
POSITIONED
PRECARIOUS

11 letters
EQUILIBRIUM
SELF-CONTROL

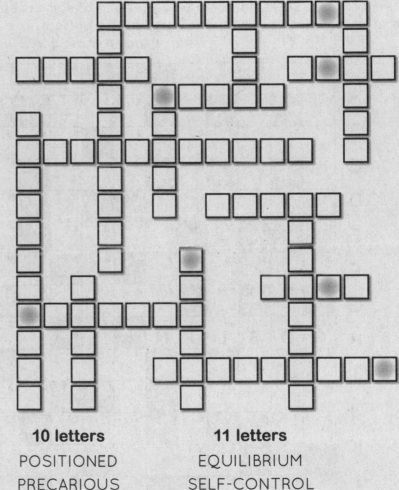

When you go surfing you might need a

__ __ __ __ __ __ __ .

13
Code Cracker

In this puzzle, you must decide which letter of the alphabet is represented by each of the numbers from 1 to 26. We have already filled in two words, so you can see that G = 20, O = 12, B = 10 and so on. Begin by repeating these letters in each box where their numbers appear in the diagram. You will then have lots of letters to help you start guessing at likely words in the grid. All the letters of the alphabet will be used, so as you decide what each one is, cross it off at the side of the grid and enter it into the reference grid at the bottom. The completed grid will look like a filled-in crossword.

14

ACROSS
1 Hot drink (3)
3 Notebook (3)
5 Written messages (7)
6 Catwalk star (5)
9 Stretchy material (7)
10 Saucepan (3)
11 Expected any time now? (3)

DOWN
1 Story (4)
2 Spaceman (9)
3 Stopped, avoided (9)
4 Short sprint (4)
7 Far down (4)
8 Measurement of land (4)

15
Storyboard

If you write the answers to these clues in the grid, reading across, you'll find that the first column spells out the title of a book. If you transfer the letters from the grid to the table below you will discover the name of the book's author.

1 Talking bird!
2 Flat, level
3 Red salad vegetable
4 Direction of sunrise
5 Hopping animal
6 Black and white 'bear'
7 A door that is slightly open is ___
8 People next door

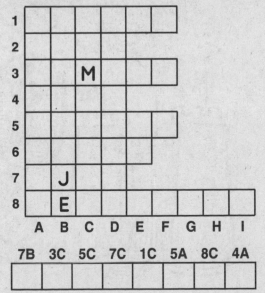

Picture This

Write the name of each item pictured into the grid, and the circled letters will spell out how Fred is spending his time.

17

ACROSS
2 Not on (3)
5 Light winds (7)
7 Tell a fib (3)
8 Twenty-four hours (3)
9 Large cushion filled with little balls (7)
10 Cardboard container (3)

DOWN
1 Period between midday and evening (9)
3 Color of grass (5)
4 Part of a bicycle (5)
5 Baby's apron (3)
6 Droop (3)

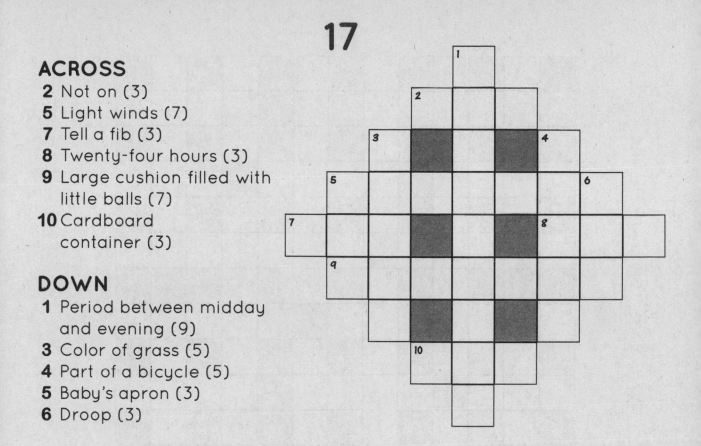

18
Take Five

The answers to these clues are all five-letter words. Enter them into the grid, reading across, and the letters in the diagonal row will spell out something spooky.

1 Grass color
2 White stick for writing on a blackboard
3 Time-telling device
4 Slack
5 Not heavy

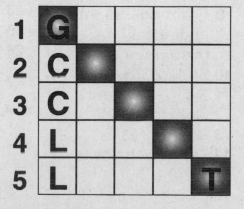

19

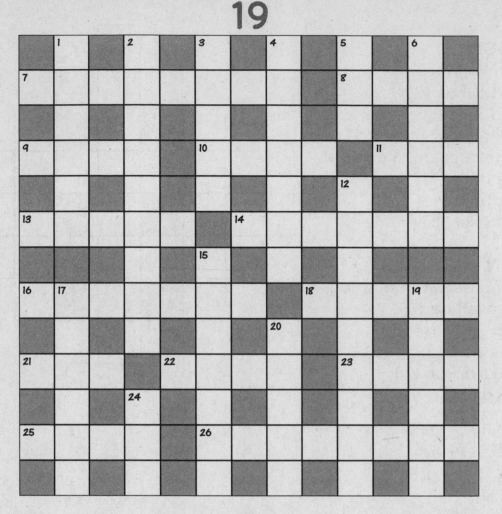

ACROSS

7 Australian mammal with a pouch (8)
8 Center of an apple (4)
9 What you might do under the mistletoe (4)
10 Sheep's fleece (4)
11 Big ___, London clocktower (3)
13 Robber (5)
14 Person who sells meat (7)
16 Deer's horns (7)
18 Warm outdoor garments (5)
21 Cook in oil (3)
22 Film celebrity (4)
23 Water ___, flower (4)
25 Young horse (4)
26 Writer of music, such as Beethoven (8)

DOWN

1 From Denmark (6)
2 Containers of yolks (9)
3 Royal headgear (5)
4 Fruit that has a white fleshy inside and a husky shell (7)
5 Highest or lowest playing card (3)
6 Light wind (6)
12 Male pupil (9)
15 Defend, shield from harm (7)
17 Not wide (6)
19 Spoke, chatted (6)
20 Tiny piece of bread (5)
24 Go by plane (3)

ACROSS

1 Go to see (5)
4 Wet boggy land (5)
7 Mass of water (3)
8 Boat paddle (3)
9 Lion's lair (3)
10 Not shut (4)
11 Fix with glue (5)
14 Pop ____, band (5)
16 Music with lyrics (4)
18 Not at home (3)
20 Tell fibs (3)
21 Frozen water (3)
22 Sporting occasion (5)
23 Imagine while asleep (5)

DOWN

1 Jar for flowers (4)
2 Hair cleaner (7)
3 Rose's prickle (5)
4 Suitcase fastener (5)
5 Help (3)
6 Small horses (6)
12 Daybreak (7)
13 Take no notice of (6)
15 Aircraft flyer (5)
16 Use money (5)
17 Roof timber (4)
19 Foot digit (3)

21
Letter Play

Try to work out where each of the three-letter words in the list fit into the grid. If you do it correctly each line of the grid will have Two six-letter words.

AGE   LAY   MIS
HIT   MAN   OUT

MIS		

22

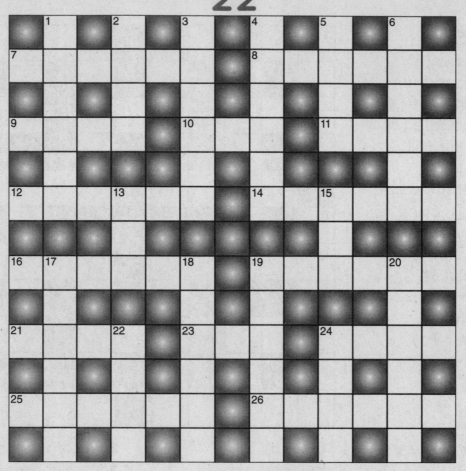

ACROSS

7 Capital city of England (6)
8 Beast, creature (6)
9 Plant stalk (4)
10 Frozen water (3)
11 Film about a talking pig (4)
12 Period of ten years (6)
14 Longest river in South America (6)
16 Grown-ups (6)
19 Set of cooking instructions (6)
21 Middle of the leg (4)
23 Circuit of a track (3)
24 Young cow (4)
25 ____ wheel, fairground attraction (6)
26 Inuit houses (6)

DOWN

1 Glass container for liquid (6)
2 Eve's partner in the Bible (4)
3 Motor (6)
4 Tool for taking photographs (6)
5 Arm or leg (4)
6 Giant tropical grass eaten by pandas (6)
13 Everything (3)
15 Part of a curve (3)
17 One who moves to music (6)
18 Sound of an object hitting water (6)
20 Bed cushion (6)
22 Make money (4)
24 Chilly (4)

Picture This

Write the name of each item pictured into the grid, and the circled letters will spell out the color the artist needs to finish his painting.

Arroword

Can you solve the puzzle? The arrows show you where to write your answers.

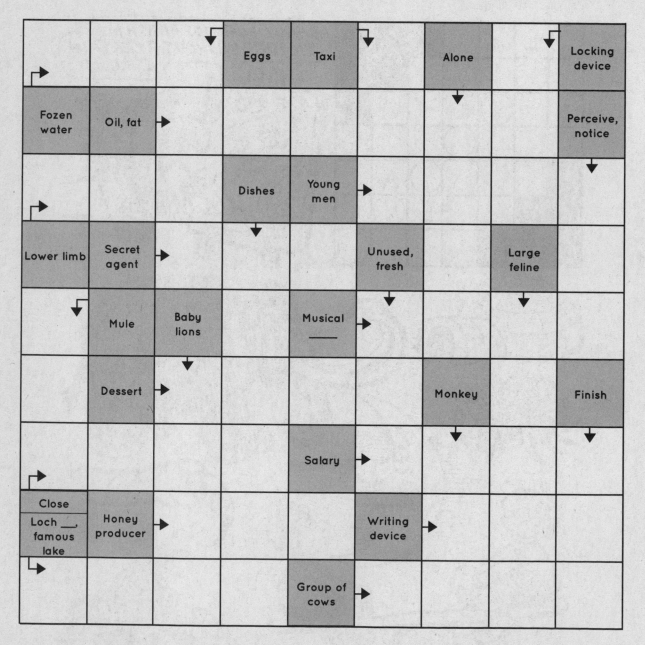

25
Cartoon Crossword

To fill in the blank crossword grid, take the first letter of each item pictured in the lower grid. For example, box 1 will contain a B as it's the first letter of bulb.

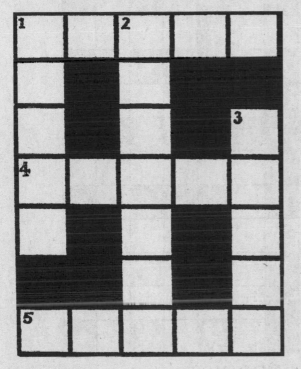

26
Word Ladder

Can you climb down the word ladder from WORK to FARM? Simply change one letter in WORK for the answer to the first clue, then one letter in that answer for the answer to the second clue, and so on.

CLUES
1 Was dressed in
2 Thin metal string
3 Flames
4 Quite hard

W	O	R	K
F	A	R	M

27

ACROSS

7 Cushion for your head (6)
8 Weight to hold a ship steady (6)
9 Dotted cubes used in playing games (4)
10 Fib (3)
11 Out of danger (4)
12 Ring (6)
14 Sofa (6)
16 Hard-backed insect (6)
19 Small shelter for a dog (6)
21 Bird's bill (4)
23 Nocturnal flying mammal (3)
24 Unable to hear (4)
25 Banana-colored (6)
26 Set of steps for climbing up and down (6)

DOWN

1 Two-piece swimsuit (6)
2 Color of the sky (4)
3 Number in a dozen (6)
4 Makers of cakes and bread (6)
5 Performs in a play (4)
6 Hot drink made from ground beans (6)
13 Feline animal (3)
15 Metal container (3)
17 Twenty minus nine (6)
18 Arm joints (6)
19 Vessel used to boil water (6)
20 Pencil ____, rubber (6)
22 Scottish national dress (4)
24 Large extinct bird (4)

28

ACROSS

1 Japanese wrestling (4)
3 Team of workers on a ship (4)
7 Male sheep (3)
8 Performed in a play (5)
9 Male person (3)
10 Which person (3)
12 Use a needle and thread (3)
14 Sportsperson, runner (7)
15 Powdery remains of a fire (3)
16 Pixie (3)
18 Honey-making insect (3)
19 Black and white bear-like animal (5)
21 Writing tool (3)
22 Munches, swallows (4)
23 Animal doctors (4)

DOWN

1 Drinking tube (5)
2 Prehistoric elephant (7)
4 Rodent associated with the Pied Piper of Hamelin (3)
5 Black ____, venomous spider (5)
6 Steering device on a bike (9)
11 Owns (3)
12 Church spire (7)
13 Long snake-like fish (3)
15 Orchard fruit such as a Grannie Smith (5)
17 Snake's teeth (5)
20 Almond or cashew, for example (3)

ACROSS

2 Precious stone (3)
4 Parts of a skeleton (5)
7 Help (3)
9 Hard black fuel burnt on a fire (4)
11 Revolve rapidly (4)
12 ___ *Baba And The Forty Theives*, story (3)
13 Go in (5)
15 Cooking and heating fuel (3)

DOWN

1 Big ___, London clock (3)
2 Young goose (7)
3 Infectious disease producing red spots (7)
5 Drink a little (3)

6 ___ constrictor, large snake (3)
8 Use a spade (3)
10 Beer (3)
14 Go brown in the sun (3)

Take Five

The answers to these clues are all five-letter words. Enter them into the grid, reading across, and the letters in the diagonal row of shaded boxes should spell out a type of fish.

1 Bamboo-eating black and white animal
2 Bicycle foot part
3 Tom and ___, cartoon duo
4 Noise made by a duck
5 Timepiece worn on the wrist

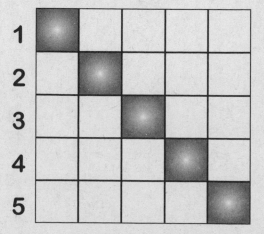

ACROSS

1 Collection of ships (5)
4 Room in the roof (5)
7 Daytime snooze (3)
8 Fluid in pens (3)
9 Cooking pot (3)
10 Thick string (4)
11 Dentist's tool (5)
14 Put on clothes (5)
16 Useless plant (4)
18 Legal code (3)
20 Chunk of firewood (3)
21 Organ for seeing (3)
22 Fable or fairy tale (5)
23 Time when we sleep (5)

DOWN

1 Locate (a lost object) (4)
2 Blow up (7)
3 Once more than once (5)
4 Inquired (5)
5 Fixture on a sink (3)

6 Light made from wick and wax (6)
12 Large glacial floating mass (7)
13 Grown-ups (6)
15 Stupid, foolish (5)
16 Horse-drawn cart (5)
17 Examination (4)
19 Dr. ____, TV time traveler (3)

32

ACROSS

1 Ice cream container (3)
5 Green-leafed salad food (7)
6 Distance from the surface to the bottom (5)
9 Policeman (7)
10 Device for unlocking a door (3)
11 ___ and bacon, breakfast favorite (3)

DOWN

1 Above average height (4)
2 Insect with large colorful wings (9)
3 Try to lose weight (4)
4 Hair on the upper lip (9)
7 Large stone (4)
8 Adult tadpole (4)

33

First Letters

In this puzzle you must answer the general knowledge questions and enter the first letter of each answer in the numbered box to reveal a glowing object.

1 Seat on a horse (6)
2 Capital of France (5)
3 Fruit of the oak tree (5)
4 Material used to make tires (6)
5 For boiling water in (6)
6 Biggest city in England (6)
7 Large bird of prey (5)
8 Dried grape (6)

1	2	3	4	5	6	7	8

34
Picture This

Write the name of each item pictured into the grid, and the circled letters will spell out what the weather is going to be like.

35

ACROSS

7 Sound level (6)
8 Fifth ____, famous Manhattan thoroughfare (6)
9 Do as you're told (4)
10 Sick (3)
11 Hit with the foot (4)
12 Sewing tool (6)
14 Filmmaker's machine (6)
16 Glues, pastes (6)
19 Spot, observe (6)
21 Mountain lion, cougar (4)
23 Alphabet (inits)(3)
24 Length of office (4)
25 Father or mother (6)
26 Web-making creature (6)

DOWN

1 Twice the amount (6)
2 Cover in earth (4)
3 Instrument, machine (6)
4 Plant with a strong taste and smell (6)
5 From Monday to Sunday (4)
6 Fruit squeezer (6)
13 What's up, ____?, Bugs Bunny's catchphrase (3)
15 *When Harry ____ Sally*, Meg Ryan film (3)
17 Bird with a large colored beak (6)
18 Begins (6)
19 Kindest (6)
20 Place where two roads meet (6)
22 Zone or region (4)
24 One of two identical people (4)

ACROSS

1 Grilled bread (5)
4 Bird with a red breast (5)
7 Automobile (3)
8 Fishing pole (3)
9 Obtain, acquire (3)
10 Spongy green plant (4)
11 American cowboy show (5)
14 More than usual (5)
16 ____ and vinegar, crisp flavor (4)
18 Fairy-like creature (3)
20 Grow older (3)
21 Jump on one leg (3)
22 Exhausted, sleepy (5)
23 Bedding items (5)

DOWN

1 Clock or watch noise (4)
2 Plane terminal (7)
3 Rubber coverings for wheels (5)
4 Aircraft location system (5)
5 Container for shopping (3)
6 People of a particular country (6)
12 Intelligent sea mammal such as Flipper (7)
13 Failure to win (6)
15 Prize such as an Oscar (5)
16 Nut's outer covering (5)
17 Not shut (4)
19 Distant, remote (3)

37

ACROSS

7 Run fast like a horse (6)

8 Animal that lives in a hutch (6)

9 Kanga's baby in Winnie-the-Pooh (3)

10 Creature with feathers (4)

11 Twelve months (4)

12 Lower limb (3)

14 Beijing's country (5)

17 Cutting part of a knife (5)

19 Bend (5)

20 Lamb's noise (5)

22 Game played with small arrows (5)

24 Doctor ____, TV time traveler (3)

26 Opposite of empty (4)

28 Badger's den (4)

29 Cooling device (3)

30 Cheddar or Stilton, for example (6)

31 Person in charge of a newspaper (6)

DOWN

1 Disappear (6)

2 Toboggan (4)

3 Fourth month (5)

4 Pointed part of a fork (5)

5 Carry out orders (4)

6 Four-legged reptile with scales (6)

13 Our planet (5)

15 Frozen water (3)

16 Take part in a play (3)

17 Sleeping place (3)

18 Substance we breathe (3)

21 Giggles (6)

23 Design painted on the skin (6)

24 Light cookie eaten with ice cream (5)

25 Possessed (5)

27 Long onion-like vegetable (4)

28 Large boat (4)

38
Code Cracker

In this puzzle, you must decide which letter of the alphabet is represented by each of the numbers from 1 to 26. We have already filled in two words, so you can see that C = 9, A = 6, and R = 7. Begin by repeating these letters in each box where their numbers appear in the diagram. You will then have lots of letters to help you start guessing at likely words in the grid. All the letters of the alphabet will be used, so as you decide what each one is, cross it off at the side of the grid and enter it into the reference grid at the bottom. The completed grid will look like a filled-in crossword.

39

ACROSS

2 Opposite of no (3)
5 Drink like a cat (3)
6 Little (5)
9 Number of seasons in a year (4)
10 Last word of a prayer (4)
12 One who travels on horseback (5)
14 Baby's bed (3)
15 Soaking (3)

DOWN

1 Prison room (4)
3 Summer dish of lettuce, tomatoes etc. (5)
4 Bird similar to an ostrich (3)
6 Weep (3)
7 Large dart (5)
8 That girl (3)
11 Cat's cry (3)
13 Thing, object (4)

40

Ladder Word

Work out where each of the three-letter words in the list fit into the grid. If you do it correctly a well known city will read down the shaded squares.

AGE   LAS
EAT   NOT
ERA   REE
ILL

P				T	I	C
F				D	O	M
M	A	N				R
A				H	E	R
W				H	E	R
G	R				E	D
M	I	N				L

41
Picture This

Write the name of each item pictured into the grid, and the circled letters will spell out a sport that's popular in England, Australia, and India.

ACROSS

2 Fishing pole (3)
5 Father (3)
6 Breakfast meat (5)
9 Cry of a wolf (4)
10 100th of a dollar (4)
12 In the lead (5)
14 Number of seats on a tandem bike (3)
15 Source of heat and light (3)

DOWN

1 Extinct bird (4)
3 Move in time to music (5)
4 Cat's foot (3)
6 Cardboard container (3)
7 Animals' sharp toenails (5)

8 Last part (3)
11 Listening organ (3)
13 Sixty minutes (4)

43

First And Last

Solve the clues and write your answers in the grid. Then read downwards to find a vegetable.

1 Board game with pawns, knights, and kings
2 Striped horse
3 Aunt's husband
4 Feather pen
5 Brainwaves, notions
6 Robber
7 Chuckle, guffaw
8 ____ jet, large plane
9 Snow color
10 Frighten
11 The Mississippi, for example

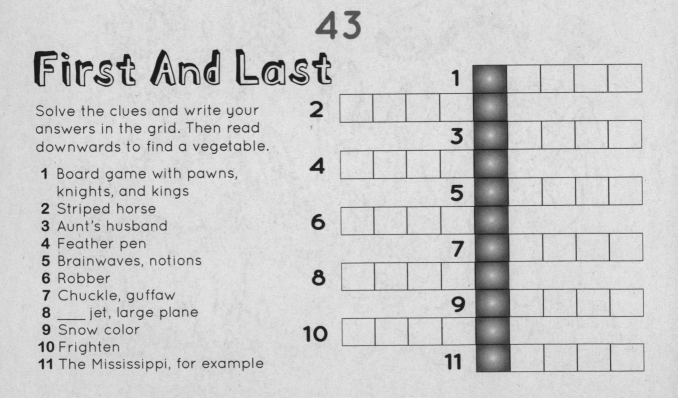

ACROSS

7 ___ L. Jackson, actor (6)
8 Toxic substance (6)
9 Hens' produce (4)
10 Past, gone (3)
11 Clock noise (4)
12 ___ of Liberty, New York landmark (6)
14 Color of a New York taxi (6)
16 *Snow White and the Seven* ___, film (6)
19 Fellow actor or actress in a film or play (2-4)
21 World's largest continent (4)
23 Expert golfer (3)
24 Twist out of shape (4)
25 Law enforcement officers (6)
26 Floppy, limp (6)

DOWN

1 Coached, tutored (6)
2 ___ Bunny, cartoon character (4)
3 Polite word of request (6)
4 Ghostly, weird (6)
5 Baseball glove (4)
6 South American cloak (6)
13 Black road-surfacing material (3)
15 ___ Vegas, US city (3)
17 Good sense and knowledge based on experience (6)
18 Last meal of the day (6)
19 Overcast, gloomy (6)
20 Sudden, unexpected (6)
22 Barren, parched (4)
24 Timber (4)

45

ACROSS

7 Salted or roasted snack (6)
8 Munching (6)
9 Solid square (4)
10 Long, slippery fish (3)
11 Hairless (4)
12 Young swan (6)
14 Come back (6)
16 Circus entertainers (6)
19 Nail-hitting tool (6)
21 Gigantic (4)
23 Hot drink made with a bag (3)
24 Price (4)
25 Shake with cold (6)
26 Pill (6)

DOWN

1 ____ and the Beast, fairy tale (6)
2 Leg joint (4)
3 Road (6)
4 Underground room (6)
5 Pierce with a knife (4)
6 Deer's horn (6)
13 This minute (3)
15 Male cat (3)
17 Chuckles (6)
18 Planet with rings (6)
19 Red suit at cards (6)
20 Simpler (6)
22 Jealousy (4)
24 Baby lions (4)

46

ACROSS
2 Go bad (3)
5 Grease (3)
6 Blood pump (5)
9 Young horse (4)
10 Allow to borrow (4)
12 Sheep's cry (5)
14 Stick for playing pool (3)
15 Cat's cry (3)

DOWN
1 Opposite of rich (4)
3 Name of a book or film (5)
4 Small round vegetable (3)
6 Jump on one leg (3)
7 Photo book (5)
8 Small insect (3)
11 Hearing organ (3)
13 Vegetable with a long white stem and broad green leaves (4)

47

Cartoon Crossword

To fill in the blank crossword grid, take the first letter of each pictured item in the grid. For example, box 1 will have an O inside it as it's the first letter of orange.

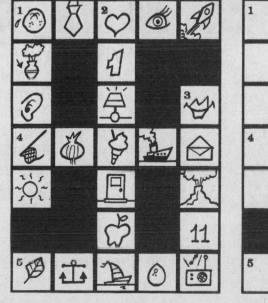

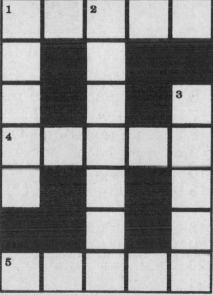

48

ACROSS

5 Tiny jumping insect (4)
6 Small round bread bun (4)
7 Hearing organ (3)
8 Poses a question (4)
9 All right (4)
10 Church symbols (7)
13 Woolen bedcover (7)
17 Rim (4)
18 Go by boat (4)
19 Small circular mark (3)
20 Breathing organ for fish (4)
21 Wicked (4)

DOWN

1 Container for holding liquid (5)
2 Julius ____, Roman ruler (6)
3 Bows and ____, archer's equipment (6)
4 Made a noise like a sheep (7)
11 Tree which grows from an acorn (3)
12 Disney character who found a magic lamp (7)
14 Sharp instrument for sewing (6)
15 Chocolate eggs time (6)
16 Small fairy (5)

49

ACROSS
1 Silky material (5)
4 Charge for work done (3)
6 Country north of Mexico (initials) (3)
8 ___fish, sushi (3)
9 Songs (5)
11 ___ up, confessed (5)
14 Use your eyes (3)
15 Single (3)
16 Conclusion (3)
17 Middle body part (5)

DOWN
1 Charles Dickens' Christmas miser (7)
2 Pull another vehicle (3)
3 Almond, for example (3)
4 Cooling device (3)
5 Simplest (7)

7 Nearest star (3)
10 Animal enclosure (3)
12 Move the head back and forth (3)
13 Morning dampness (3)
14 Go downhill fast on snow (3)

50

Egg Timer

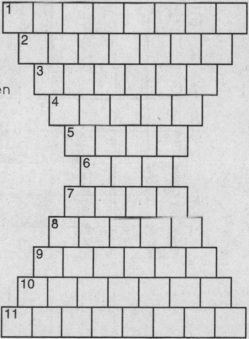

To solve this puzzle you have to remove a letter from the previous answer and (if necessary) rearrange the letters to get the new answer. When you pass clue 6, you have to do the opposite - adding a letter each time.

1 Chirping insects (8)
2 Adhesive label (7)
3 Baseball term for a missed hit (6)
4 Female garment (5)
5 Hazard (4)
6 Go downhill fast on snow (3)
7 Disappear under water (4)
8 _ of Leon, US rock group (5)
9 Requesting or inquiring (6)
10 Activity on the ice (7)
11 Heaping up (8)

Code Cracker

In this puzzle, you must decide which letter of the alphabet is represented by each of the numbers from 1 to 26. We have already filled in two words, so you can see that H = 26, O = 19, T = 18 and so on. Begin by repeating these letters in each box where their numbers appear in the diagram. You will then have lots of letters to help you start guessing at likely words in the grid. All the letters of the alphabet will be used, so as you decide what each one is, cross it off at the side of the grid and enter it into the reference grid at the bottom. The completed puzzle will look like a filled-in crossword.

4	13	2	3	17	■	1	■	7	19	3	17	■	2	■
13	■	1	■	2	■	2	20	17	■	■	12	25	18	26
2	24	19	5	21	10	18	■	10	25	6	17	■	18	■
23	■	11	■	9	■	26 H	19 O	18 T	■	17	■	18	25	8
18	17	17	16	17	17	■	■	17	24	1	23	2	8	17
17	■	■	2	■	2	7	2	23	■	23	■	20	■	22
23	13	5	5	17	23	■	1	■	5	2	18	25	11	17
■	10	■	22	■	18	2	1	9	17	■	23	■	2	■
22	17	18	2	8	26	■	19	■	25	21	13	2	5	2
17	■	17	■	26	■	10	18	2	21	■	10	■	■	17
2	10	10	2	13	9	18	■	■	26	2	18	18	17	23
15	2	18	■	5	■	13	23	5 N	■	9	■	12	■	19
■	9	■	10	3	25	22	■	25 I	9	9	5	17	10	10
9	2	11	2	■	■	25	5	5 N	■	17	■	17	■	19
■	22	■	22	19	22	19	■	17 E	■	14	19	22	17	9

A B C D E F G H I J K L M

N O P Q R S T U V W X Y Z

1	2	3	4	5	6	7	8	9	10	11	12	13
				N								

14	15	16	17	18	19	20	21	22	23	24	25	26
			E	T	O						I	H

52
Picture This

Write the name of each item pictured into the grid, and the circled letters will spell out what the chef is going to make.

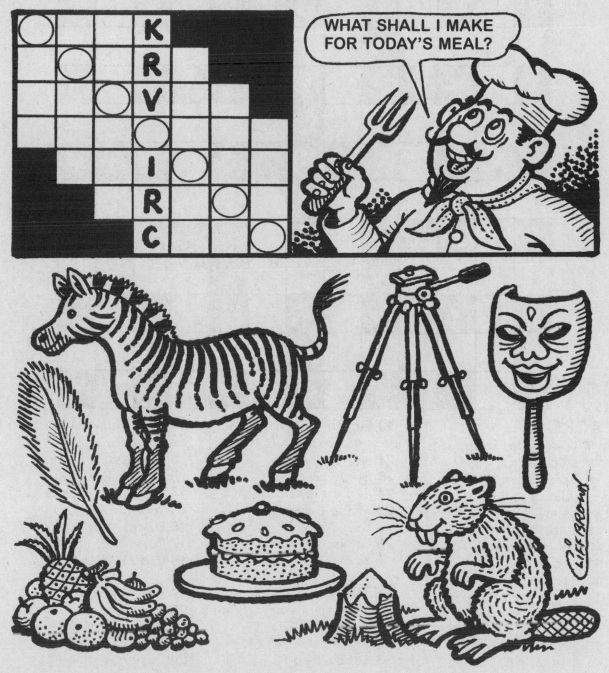

53

ACROSS

7 Weight for holding a ship steady (6)
8 Color produced by mixing red and yellow (6)
9 Unable to hear (4)
10 Dawn moisture (3)
11 Trickle (4)
12 Horse's shelter (6)
14 Someone who makes an offer at an auction (6)
16 Medical man or woman (6)
19 Eighth month of the year (6)
21 Not shut (4)
23 Small piece (3)
24 Explosive weapon (4)
25 African wildlife tour (6)
26 Chocolate and cream pastry puff (6)

DOWN

1 Ant, fly, or earwig, for example (6)
2 Head cook (4)
3 Baby's bed (6)
4 Fine network spun by a spider (6)
5 Hairless (4)
6 Set on fire (6)
13 Nocturnal flying mammal (3)
15 Use a spade (3)
17 Parentless child (6)
18 Who Framed Roger ___?, film (6)
19 Stag's horn (6)
20 Highest point on a mountain (6)
22 Tidy (4)
24 Daring, brave (4)

ACROSS

2 Baby's apron (3)
5 Movement of a tail (3)
6 What a conjurer uses (5)
9 Washtub (4)
10 Egg-shaped (4)
12 Possessor (5)
14 Function, purpose (3)
15 Knock gently (3)

DOWN

1 Exotic fruit or New Zealand bird (4)
3 Breakfast meat (5)
4 Feline animal (3)
6 Area diagram (3)
7 Phantom (5)
8 Glass container (3)
11 Animal doctor (3)
13 Not strong (4)

55

Kite Words

In this puzzle, you must solve the clues and then fit the answers into the kite, reading across. We've filled in the first letters of the answers and the solution to one clue to help you decide where they all fit, and the length of each answer should give you a clue. If you do this correctly, the letters in the center column will spell out a type of food.

Large (3)
Not happy (3)
Comical (5)
Use your nose (5)
In need of a drink (7)
Mischievous (7)
~~Capital city of Scotland (9)~~
Australian curved throwing stick (9)
Power for TV, fridge, etc. (11)

56

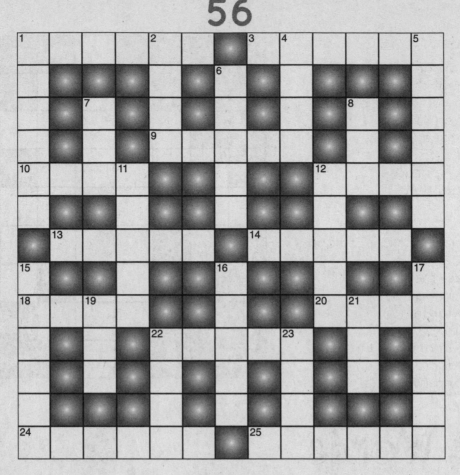

ACROSS

1 Bows and ____, weapons (6)
3 Type of grass eaten by pandas (6)
9 Sweet substance made by bees (5)
10 Sodium chloride (4)
12 Tiny jumping insect (4)
13 Group of sheep (5)
14 Digging tool (5)
18 Complain, whine (4)
20 Flying toy (4)
22 One of the gifts presented by the Three Wise Men (5)
24 Male relation (6)
25 ____ Duck, Disney character (6)

DOWN

1 Type of crossword clue (6)
2 Made when blowing out candles on a birthday cake (4)
4 Go ____, leave a place (4)
5 Bandit (6)
6 ____ Claus, Father Christmas (5)
7 Wise bird (3)
8 Not well (3)
11 Sharp point on a rose stem (5)
12 Container for keeping liquid hot or cold (5)
15 Second longest river (6)
16 Christmas song (5)
17 Shouted (6)
19 Perform in a play (3)
21 Frozen water (3)
22 Rodents (4)
23 Ring above an angel's head (4)

57
Code Cracker

In this puzzle, you must decide which letter of the alphabet is represented by each of the numbers 1 to 26. We have already filled in two words, so you can see that C = 8, I = 17, T = 19, and Y = 16, and so on. Begin by repeating these letters in each box where their numbers appear in the diagram. You will then have lots of letters to help you start guessing at likely words in the grid. All the letters of the alphabet will be used, so as you decide what each one is, cross it off at the side of the grid and enter it into the reference grid at the bottom. The completed grid will look like a filled-in crossword.

1	2	3	4	5	6	7	8	9	10	11	12	13
B							C					
14	15	16	17	18	19	20	21	22	23	24	25	26
	A	Y	I		T							

58

ACROSS
2 Jump on one leg (3)
5 Tree which grows from an acorn (3)
6 Color of army uniforms (5)
9 Big cat (4)
10 Dark blue (4)
12 Small cat (5)
14 Ancient (3)
15 Snake-like fish (3)

DOWN
1 Paperback (4)
3 Artist's colored liquid (5)
4 Dr. ___, TV time-traveler (3)
6 Young goat (3)
7 Foot joint (5)
8 Evergreen climbing plant (3)
11 Munched (3)
13 Brainwave (4)

59

First And Last

Solve the anagrams with the help of the clues and write your answers in the grid reading across. If you do this correctly, the first and last letters will spell out a fun place to visit.

1 FORO — House covering
2 MAAD — ___ and Eve, first man and woman
3 MIIN — Small car
4 SORB — Steals
5 GRIN — Circle
6 MORO — Space
7 OLSO — Performance for one person
8 NOUD — Unfasten
9 IHNT — Slim
10 WOND — Opposite of up

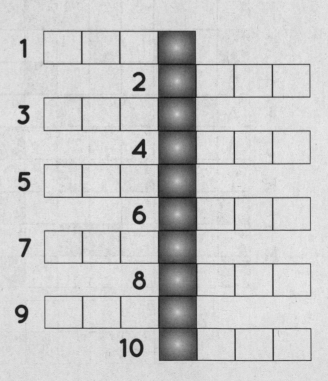

60

ACROSS

5 White flakes (4)
6 Remove creases in clothes (4)
7 Item laid by a hen (3)
8 Toy human (4)
9 Large pool (4)
10 One hundred years (7)
13 Prickly plant, emblem of Scotland (7)
17 ____ Halliwell, ex-Spice Girl (4)
18 One of two babies born at the same time (4)
19 Speck (3)
20 Lion's hair (4)
21 Opposite of early (4)

DOWN

1 Be nosy, pry (5)
2 Number in a dozen (6)
3 Baby farm animal with a snout (6)
4 Storage compartments for clothes at a gym (7)
11 Almond, brazil, or pistachio, for example (3)
12 Spotted cat, the fastest animal on land (7)
14 Web-spinner (6)
15 Small (6)
16 Presents (5)

61

ACROSS

7 Breakfast food (6)
8 Writer (6)
9 Yogi ____, cartoon character (4)
10 Animal doctor (3)
11 Place where money is saved (4)
12 Pearl-producing sea creature (6)
14 Twenty times four (6)
16 Mother or father (6)
19 Tool for banging in nails (6)
21 Sketch (4)
23 Olive ____, Popeye's girlfriend (3)
24 Young horse (4)
25 Capture and hold for ransom (6)
26 Number in a soccer team (6)

DOWN

1 Long, crunchy vegetable (6)
2 Fruit shaped like a lightbulb (4)
3 Smart, intelligent (6)
4 Cows (6)
5 Pierce with a knife (4)
6 Easter hat (6)
13 Part of the foot (3)
15 Jewel (3)
17 Scared (6)
18 Soldiers (6)
19 Protective headwear (6)
20 Pencil rubber (6)
22 Magician's stick (4)
24 Tiny, jumping insect (4)

62
Picture This

Write the name of each item pictured into the grid, and the circled letters will spell out what the boy is going to do on vacation.

63

ACROSS
7 Limb of a tree (6)
8 Color of carrots (6)
9 Muck (4)
10 Long, slippery fish (3)
11 Skinny (4)
12 Horse's home (6)
14 Tennis equipment (6)
16 Light made from wick and wax (6)
19 Men's hairdresser (6)
21 Scuttling crustacean with claws (4)
23 Male sheep (3)
24 Strong cord (4)
25 Two-piece swimsuit (6)
26 Rectangle (6)

DOWN
1 Painter or sculptor, for example (6)
2 Small biting fly (4)
3 Cheddar or Stilton, for example (6)
4 American currency (6)
5 Speedy (4)
6 Set fire to (6)
13 Naughty (3)
15 Automobile (3)
17 Scared (6)
18 Small insect with pincers (6)
19 Giant panda's food (6)
20 Grow larger (6)
22 Cook in hot water (4)
24 Bread bun (4)

64

ACROSS
5 Number of digits on one hand (4)
6 Dull pain (4)
7 Everything (3)
8 Sound made by a snake (4)
9 Uncle's wife (4)
10 Very old (7)
13 Large cushion filled with polystyrene balls (7)
17 Compact ____, music device (4)
18 Go yachting (4)
19 Neckwear (3)
20 Molten stream from a volcano (4)
21 Short letter (4)

DOWN
1 Pay a call (5)
2 Autumn or spring, for example (6)
3 Spicy Italian sausage (6)
4 Gleaming (7)
11 Male swan (3)
12 Water bird with large, pouched beak (7)
14 Sweet liquid sought by bees (6)
15 Away, not present (6)
16 Half of a hundred (5)

65

Word Ladder

Can you climb down the word ladder from WARM to COOL? Simply change one letter in WARM for the answer to the first clue, then one letter in that answer for the answer to the second clue, and so on.

CLUES
1) Grub, maggot
2) Shape
3) Small castle
4) 12 inches
5) Jester

W	A	R	M
1			
2			
3			
4			
5			
C	O	O	L

3 letters
AIM
EMU
EVE
FAT

5 letters
APPLE
AREAS
DRAPE
EQUIP
EXPEL
OUTER

RATIO
THUMB
TRAIT

6 letters
OYSTER
SIPPED
TACKLE
WANDER

7 letters
CIRCUIT
EASTERN

ENTREAT
FITNESS
LARGELY
LEGIBLE
ROMANCE
TEENAGE

9 letters
ARROGANCE
PRECEDENT

11 letters
INTERPRETER

67

ACROSS
7 Long knife (6)
8 Dried grape (6)
9 Remain (4)
10 Mesh for catching fish (3)
11 Water bird (4)
12 Gentle wind (6)
14 Small reddish salad vegetable (6)
16 Seabird with a brightly-colored beak (6)
19 Heavenly ____, the sun, moon, and stars (6)
21 Whirl (4)
23 Perform on stage (3)
24 Silver paper (4)
25 Go on a journey (6)
26 Not very wide (6)

DOWN
1 Crispy coating for fried fish (6)
2 Unattractive, like Cinderella's sisters (4)
3 Third place medal in the Olympics (6)
4 Mouth of a volcano (6)
5 Feathered creature (4)
6 Big Top entertainment (6)
13 Small fairy (3)
15 Father (3)
17 Referee (6)
18 Almost (6)
19 Study of plants (6)
20 Magazine chief (6)
22 Dark blue (4)
24 Piece of cutlery with prongs (4)

Code Cracker

In this puzzle, you must decide which letter of the alphabet is represented by each of the numbers from 1 to 26. We have already filled in two words, so you can see that S = 19, K = 1, I = 15, and so on. Begin by repeating these letters in each box where their numbers appear in the diagram. You will then have lots of letters to help you start guessing at likely words in the grid. All the letters of the alphabet will be used, so as you decide what each one is, cross it off at the side of the grid and enter it into the reference grid at the bottom.

The completed puzzle will look like a filled-in crossword.

A B C D E F G H I J K L M

12	21	18	21	25	■	25	■	7	5	17	20	■	20	■
20	■	15	■	21	■	21	16	26	■	■	16	20	22	21
6	20	9	22	20	15	17	■	13	15	6	21	■	25	■
1	■	21	■	11	■	19 S	1 K	15 I	■	26	■	4	20	22
13	20	24	1	21	17	■	■	4	10	24	17	15	19	3
20	■	■	3	■	10	16	25	5	■	16	■	2	■	10
18	15	2	20	24	13	■	20	■	2	15	16	2	20	16
■	6	■	1	■	16	26	24	19	21	■	24	■	24	■
13	21	4	15	17	21	■	16	■	23	25	21	20	6	3
21	■	10	■	26	■	19	21	21	24	■	20	■	■	26
20	6	24	26	23	20	22	■	■	20 A	6 C	22 T	15 I	26 O	17 N
4	25	5	■	25	■	20	14	21	■	20	■	13	■	21
■	26	■	19	21	21	9	■	13	21	9	24	21	19	19
8	10	15	22	■	■	25	21	16	■	21	■	20	■	22
■	13	■	5	26	1	21	■	21	■	24	20	25	25	5

N O P Q R S T U V W X Y Z

1	2	3	4	5	6	7	8	9	10	11	12	13
K					C							

14	15	16	17	18	19	20	21	22	23	24	25	26
	I		N		S	A		T				O

Ladder Word

Work out where each of the three letter words in the list fit into the grid. If you do it correctly, a well known city will read down the shaded squares.

APT   SAG
ASH   SEA
LEM   TIE
REM

P				I	E	R
D	I			S	E	
E			E	N	T	
C	H			E	R	
F			I	O	N	
P	A			N	T	
M	E	S			E	

Lose-A-Letter

If you solve these clues and fit the answers into the boxes, you'll see that the words in the right-hand column contain the same letters as those in the left-hand column minus one letter. Write each missing letter in the shaded column and, if you solve the puzzle correctly, you'll see a sporty item reading down that column. All the words in the left-hand column contain five letters.

1 Ten minus three
2 Not odd
3 Home, dwelling
4 Garden watering tube
5 Football or soccer, for example
6 ___ and pans, kitchenware
7 Turned to ice
8 Nil
9 Lamb's noise
10 Opposite of early
11 Sunday meat cooked in the oven
12 Twinkling body in the night sky
13 European country, capital Madrid
14 Turn round quickly
15 Fast, swift
16 Handed over money
17 Male duck
18 Garden tool for removing leaves

71

ACROSS

7 Cup's dish (6)
8 Cowardly color (6)
9 Large extinct bird (4)
10 Friend, buddy (3)
11 Stinging insect (4)
12 Snoozing (6)
14 Capital city of Ireland (6)
16 Opposite of top (6)
19 Quicker (6)
21 Mail (4)
23 Used a chair (3)
24 Dog's sound (4)
25 Weight for holding a ship steady (6)
26 Chocolate ____, long cream puff (6)

DOWN

1 Well-known (6)
2 Bounced sound (4)
3 Stumble (4, 2)
4 Went by bike (6)
5 Crab's leg (4)
6 Art of growing miniature trees in pots (6)
13 Munch (3)
15 Public transport vehicle (3)
17 Large seas (6)
18 Sadness (6)
19 Mother's husband (6)
20 Pincered insect (6)
22 Roald ____, author of *Charlie and the Chocolate factory* (4)
24 Brave (4)

72
Picture This

Write the name of each item pictured into the grid, and the circled letters will spell out the name of the wild flower the girl is searching for.

73

ACROSS

5 Set of two (4)
6 Not handsome (4)
7 Organ of hearing (3)
8 Plunge into water (4)
9 Finger jewelry (4)
10 Marine plant (7)
13 Hen (7)
17 Revolve rapidly (4)
18 Go yachting (4)
19 Female rabbit (3)
20 Part of a shoe (4)
21 Baby sheep (4)

DOWN

1 Ship's room (5)
2 Light wind (6)
3 Rabbit's tunnel (6)
4 Woolen bedcover (7)
11 Noah's ship (3)
12 Section of a book (7)
14 Light made of wax (6)
15 Artists stands (6)
16 Movies (5)

74

Ladder Word

Work out where each of the three-letter words in the list fit into the grid. If you do it correctly a well known city will read down the shaded squares.

EAT	RIB
INK	RON
OWE	TIS

C	A				B	E	A	N
A	S	T			A	U	T	
S	A				F	I	E	D
B	R				H	I	N	G
H	A	L	L			E	N	
S	P	R				L	E	S

75

3 letters
ACT
DIN
LIE
WAG

5 letters
ADAPT
ATTIC
CADET
MIDGE
OUTDO
PROBE

SOLID
STOOP
TENSE

6 letters
COSMOS
LEAGUE
SWATHE
YACHTS

7 letters
AWESOME
BLATANT

DECLINE
HOSTESS
LIBRARY
PROVERB
SANDBAG
WEDDING

9 letters
ABOLITION
OVERSHOOT

11 letters
COMPILATION

Code Cracker

In this puzzle, you must decide which letter of the alphabet is represented by each of the numbers from 1 to 26. We have already filled in two words, so you can see that J = 12, A = 23, C = 25, and so on. Begin by repeating these letters in each box where their numbers appear in the diagram. You will then have lots of letters to help you start guessing at likely words in the grid. All the letters of the alphabet will be used, so as you decide what each one is, cross it off at the side of the grid and enter it into the reference grid at the bottom. The completed puzzle will look like a filled-in crossword.

Left side labels (top to bottom): A B C D E F G H I J K L M

Right side labels (top to bottom): N O P Q R S T U V W X Y Z

Main grid (■ = shaded/blank cell):

12 (J)	26	10	4	6	■	23	■	4	23	17	4	■	20	■
23 (A)	■	4	■	24	■	21 (M)	23 (A)	6 (D)	■	■	11	4	17	2
25 (C)	23	8	8	23	9	■	20	6	5	4	■	■	17	■
10 (K)	■	23	■	19	■	1	20	8	■	4	■	3	18	17
3 (P)	4	8	8	5	4	■	■	5	4	23	16	5	4	2
26 (O)	■	■	18	■	1	23	21	4	■	17	■	4	■	23
2 (T)	23	8	5	4	2	■	26	■	17	2	4	23	6	7
■	9	■	9	■	4	15	2	24	23	■	22	■	20	■
21	4	■	4	26	24	■	2	■	5	26	18	1	9	4
23	■	26	■	5	■	17	26	16	23	■	23	■	■	5
13	20	5	5	20	26	1	■	■	6	20	5	18	2	4
4	1	6	■	11	■	23	17	17	■	25	■	1	■	21
■	6	■	13	4	17	2	■	19	14	20	17	2	5	4
13	4	24	26	■	■	25	■	23	■	1	■	20	■	1
■	15	■	26	18	25	14	■	3	■	9	24	4	23	2

Reference grid:

1	2	3	4	5	6	7	8	9	10	11	12	13
	T	P			D				K		J	
14	**15**	**16**	**17**	**18**	**19**	**20**	**21**	**22**	**23**	**24**	**25**	**26**
							M		A		C	O

77

ACROSS

1 Soft wet earth (3)
3 ___ *Goes the Weasel,* nursery rhyme (3)
5 Thousands of years old (7)
6 Thinking organ (5)
9 Person undergoing hospital treatment (7)
10 ___ off, fall asleep (3)
11 Pull with a rope (3)

DOWN

1 Breakfast, lunch, or dinner (4)
2 Painted and papered (a house) (9)
3 Title given to America's leader (9)
4 Track for pedestrians or bikes (4)
7 Turn round fast (4)
8 Meat and vegetables cooked slowly in liquid (4)

78

Cartoon Crossword

To fill in the blank crossword grid, take the first letter of each pictured item in the grid. For example, box 1 will have a S inside it as it's the first letter of sack.

79

ACROSS

5 Large woody plant (4)
6 Press clothes (4)
7 Tip of a pen (3)
8 Place for baking (4)
9 Naked (4)
10 Woolen bedcover (7)
13 Young hen (7)
17 Not closed (4)
18 Very strong wind (4)
19 Fire remains (3)
20 Fifty-two weeks (4)
21 Not false (4)

DOWN

1 Courageous (5)
2 Small shelter for a dog (6)
3 Ape with very long arms (6)
4 Voyage (7)
11 Noah's ship (3)
12 Section of a book (7)
14 Yellow singing bird (6)
15 Four times twenty (6)
16 Book of photos (5)

80
Letter Play

Try to work out where each of the three-letter words in the list fit into the grid. If you do it correctly, each line of the grid will have two six-letter words.

BAT   DED   MIT
COM   HER   TEN

	BAT	

81
Picture This

Write the name of each item pictured into the grid, and the circled letters will spell out the boy's birthday.

82

ACROSS

7 Next to (6)
8 Not injured (6)
9 Wind instrument (4)
10 Part of the mouth (3)
11 Body parts used to see (4)
12 Shouted loudly (6)
14 Finally choose (6)
16 Tiny room (6)
19 Average (6)
21 Actors in a play or film (4)
23 Viral infection (3)
24 Clean with soap and water (4)
25 Harsh, strict (6)
26 Fabulous, great (6)

DOWN

1 Lacking strength and energy (6)
2 Hours, minutes, and seconds (4)
3 Closed up (6)
4 Leapt into the air (6)
5 Covering for the foot (4)
6 Buddy (6)
13 ___ Angeles, Californian city (3)
15 Cape ___, sandy peninsula in Massachusetts (3)
17 One who goes first (6)
18 Chewy caramel (6)
19 Chilled dessert (6)
20 Hesitant, not certain (6)
22 Bound with rope (4)
24 Shed tears (4)

83

ACROSS
1 Remains of a fire (3)
3 Morning moisture (3)
5 Odd, peculiar (7)
6 Variety of cloth (5)
9 Precious stone (7)
10 Hole of a needle (3)
11 Look at (3)

DOWN
1 As well (4)
2 Violent windstorm (9)
3 Unsafe (9)
4 Wild, unwanted plant (4)
7 Lazy (4)
8 Outer rim (4)

84

Egg Timer

To solve this puzzle, you have to remove a letter from the previous answer and (if necessary) rearrange the letters to get the new answer. When you pass clue 6, you have to do the opposite - adding a letter each time.

1 Woodwind instrument (8)
2 In the middle (7)
3 Hypnotic state resembling sleep (6)
4 Provide food and drink (5)
5 Drop of liquid from the eye (4)
6 (They) exist (3)
7 At the back (4)
8 Person looking after others (5)
9 Hole on the Moon (6)
10 Place producing nuclear energy (7)
11 Inventors, makers (8)

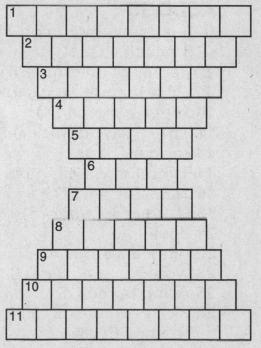

85

ACROSS

7 Australian mammal with a pouch (8)
8 Center of an apple (4)
9 Sound made by a snake (4)
10 Sheep's fleece (4)
11 Big ____, London clock (3)
13 Robber (5)
14 Person who sells meat (7)
16 Deer's horns (7)
18 Sturdy footwear (5)
21 Cook in oil (3)
22 Film celebrity (4)
23 Water ____, flower (4)
25 Young horse (4)
26 Writer of music, such as Beethoven (8)

DOWN

1 Disappear (6)
2 Containers of yolks (9)
3 Royal headgear (5)
4 Fruit that has a white fleshy inside and a husky shell (7)
5 Highest or lowest playing card (3)
6 Light wind (6)
12 Male pupil (9)
15 Defend, shield from harm (7)
17 Not wide (6)
19 Spoke, chatted (6)
20 Tiny piece of bread (5)
24 Go by plane (3)

86

3 letters
COD
MUD
OWN
PET

5 letters
ASSET
DREAM
INNER
PRIOR
READY
STRAW

TIGER
TIMER
WASTE

6 letters
EDITOR
GYRATE
PEPPER
STANCE

7 letters
CARTOON
ENCRYPT

IMMERSE
ORIGAMI
PENNANT
PROLONG
REDHEAD
RESPECT

9 letters
INNOCENCE
SKELETONS

11 letters
UNDISGUISED

87
Code Cracker

In this puzzle, you must decide which letter of the alphabet is represented by each of the numbers from 1 to 26. We have already filled in two words, so you can see that F = 21, A = 11, L = 4, and so on. Begin by repeating these letters in each box where their numbers appear in the diagram. You will then have lots of letters to help you start guessing at likely words in the grid. All the letters of the alphabet will be used, so as you decide what each one is, cross it off at the side of the grid and enter it into the reference grid at the bottom. The completed grid will look like a filled-in crossword.

A	1	2	3	2	4		5		6	7	8	9		10	
	11		11		2		2	5	7			12	13	11	4
B	14	4	8	5	11	15	2		11	4	16	12		16	
C	17		16		16		15	11	18		11		19	8	20
D	19	12	15	11	15	12			18		**F**21	**A**11	**L**4	**S**16	**E**2
E	12			22		14	8	15	23		2		11		22
F	**T**15	**A**11	**N**22	**G**20	**L**4	**E**2		11		12	18	11	22	20	2
G		20		2		11	4	4	12	3		10		2	
H	20	12	10	4	8	22		12		22	12	12	24	4	2
I	11		11		24		17	22	2	2		7			
J	15	11	16	15	2		11			18	12	15	15	2	22
K	2	4	17		11		18	7	22		25		2		
L		15		21	4	2	11		2	14	4	8	19	16	2
M	26	2	18	2			15	11	25		8		2		
		18		2	24	20	2		15		19	4	2	11	15

A B C D E F G H I J K L M — N O P Q R S T U V W X Y Z

1	2	3	4	5	6	7	8	9	10	11	12	13
	E		L							A		

14	15	16	17	18	19	20	21	22	23	24	25	26
	T	S				G	F	N				

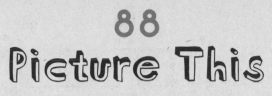

88
Picture This

To fill in the blank crossword grid, take the first letter of each item pictured in the top grid. For example, box 1 will have a B inside as it's the first letter of Bone.

ACROSS

5 Long-necked, graceful bird (4)
6 Not shut (4)
7 Metal can (3)
8 Sign of an old wound (4)
9 Small amphibian with a tail (4)
10 Part of a bird's plumage (7)
13 Bubble on the skin caused by tight shoes (7)
17 Metal button (4)
18 Not at home (4)
19 Rather dark (3)
20 Take skin off fruit (4)
21 Simple (4)

DOWN

1 Two times (5)
2 False (6)
3 Easter hat (6)
4 Marine plant (7)
11 Small, termite-like insect (3)
12 Flap quickly, like a butterfly (7)
14 Leather seat for a horse rider (6)
15 Tooth covering (6)
16 Boggy land (5)

90

Add-A-Letter

To solve this puzzle you have to add a letter to the previous answer and (if necessary) rearrange the letters to get the new answer.

1 Chew and swallow (3)
2 Opening in a fence (4)
3 Large or important (5)
4 Shredded (cheese, e.g.) (6)
5 Very sad event (7)
6 Prepared yourself (3,5)

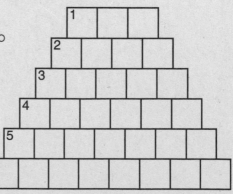

91

ACROSS

7 Space rock (6)
8 Warm up (food, e.g.) again (6)
9 Ray of light (4)
10 Go brown in the sun (3)
11 Destiny (4)
12 Instrument for writing or
drawing (6)
14 Thick dairy product (6)
16 Make equal, balance out (4,2)
19 Stopped working (6)
21 Comfortable and warm (4)
23 Bathing vessel (3)
24 Stepped (on) (4)
25 Very serious (6)
26 Enthusiasm, vitality (6)

DOWN

1 Remove (a computer file, e.g.) (6)
2 Set of players (4)
3 Savage (6)
4 Cognac (6)
5 Restaurant cook (4)
6 Server in a restaurant (6)
13 Am able to (3)
15 Neon or helium, e.g. (3)
17 Seller (6)
18 Glossy leather (6)
19 Stretchy substance (6)
20 Plenty, ample (6)
22 High-school series starring
Matthew Morrison (4)
24 Source of wood (4)

Ladder Word

Work out where each of the three letter words in the list fit into the grid. If you do it correctly, a well known city will read down the shaded squares.

AND	LIV
CHE	ONG
ERR	PER

A	B			▓	O	N	E	D
O	R			▓	S	T	R	A
S	T	R		▓		E	S	T
D	E			▓	E	R	E	D
D	E	S		▓		A	T	E
I	N	T		▓		U	P	T

ACROSS

1 *Gulliver's* ____, book by Defoe (7)
5 Snatch (4)
8 Jeans material
10 ____ match, not on home ground (4)
11 Tire slips (5)
12 Ships' floors (5)
14 Jumping insect (4)
15 Beam with pleasure (5)
17 Seldom seen (4)
18 Homes for dogs (7)

DOWN

1 Sea movement (4)
2 Girl's name (3)
3 Rough-leaved tall tree (3)
4 Shoes and ____, footwear (5)
6 Squabbles (4)
7 Spend money (3)
9 Brainwave (4)
10 ____ and Eve, bible couple (4)
11 Animal that makes a foul smell (5)
12 Animal like Bambi (4)
13 Hooks for hanging coats (4)
14 Distant (3)
15 Male child (3)
16 Skating surface (3)

94
Cartoon Crossword

To fill in the blank crossword grid, take the first letter of each pictured item in the grid. For example, box 1 will have an F inside it as it's the first letter of Fly.

95
Add-A-Letter

To solve this puzzle you have to add a letter to the previous answer and (if necessary) rearrange the letters to get the new answer.

1 Unhappy (3)
2 Hurry along (4)
3 Area protected from the sun (5)
4 Divided (between) (6)
5 (Of a computer) failed suddenly (7)
6 Looked carefully (8)

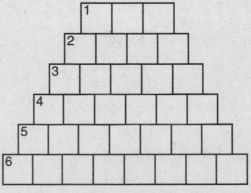

3 letters
AID
ARM
USE
VIE

5 letters
CHAFE
EPOCH
GAMMA
PLACE
RESIT
SPICE

SWEAT

6 letters
BANDIT
ENAMEL
STICKY
TROPIC

7 letters
AMMONIA
CADENCE
IMPROVE
KETCHUP

LOGICAL
PATTERN
UNTRIED
VOLTAGE

9 letters
ATTENTIVE
IMPETUOUS

11 letters
HOSPITALITY

Picture This

Write the name of each item pictured into the grid, and the circled letters will spell out the name of the magician.

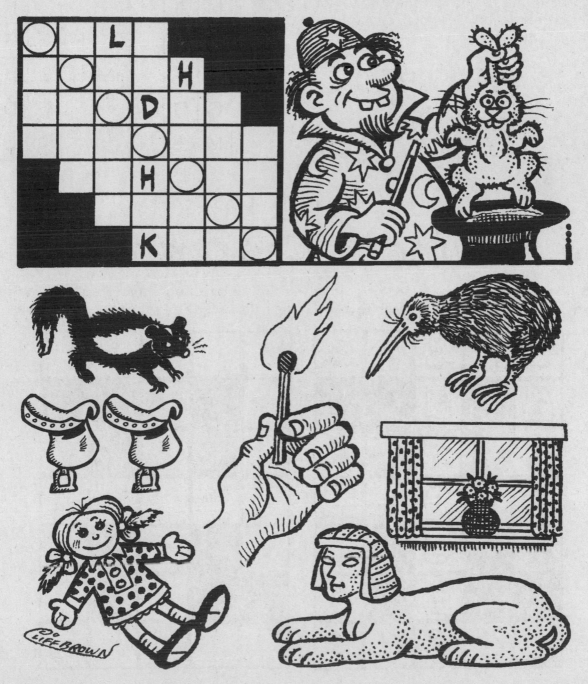

98

Ladder Word

Work out where each of the three letter words in the list fit into the grid. If you do it correctly, a well known city will read down the shaded squares.

AGE   LAS
EAT   NOT
ERA   REE
ILL

P				T	I	C
F				D	O	M
M	A	N				R
A				H	E	R
W				H	E	R
G	R				E	D
M	I	N				L

99

Cartoon Crossword

To fill in the blank crossword grid, take the first letter of each pictured item in the grid. For example, box 1 will have a T inside it as it's the first letter of triangle.

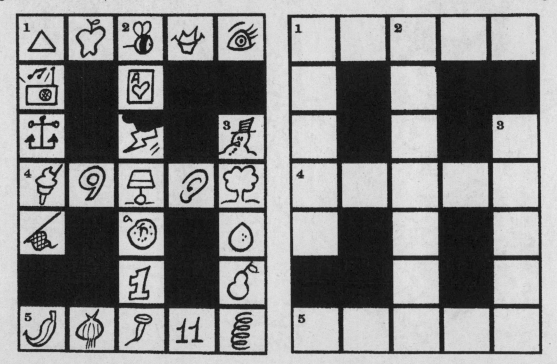

ACROSS

1 Children's magazine (5)
4 Airplane driver (5)
7 Public transport vehicle (3)
8 Help, relief (3)
9 Come first (in a race) (3)
10 Face-covering (4)
11 Maker's name inside clothing (5)
14 Smell, perfume (5)
16 Source of water (4)
18 Human limb (3)
20 Came face to face with (3)
21 Frying liquid (3)
22 Put a stop to (5)
23 Produce from bees (5)

DOWN

1 Rubik's ____, toy (4)
2 Information passed on (7)
3 Blackboard writing implement (5)
4 Bicycle ____, place for your foot! (5)
5 Legal system (3)
6 Unruly knot (6)
12 Party decoration that can be popped (7)
13 Break out of jail (6)
15 Very shy (5)
16 Timer worn on the wrist (5)
17 Take part in a game (4)
19 Wet sticky earth (3)

101
Arroword

Write the answers into the squares shown by the arrows.

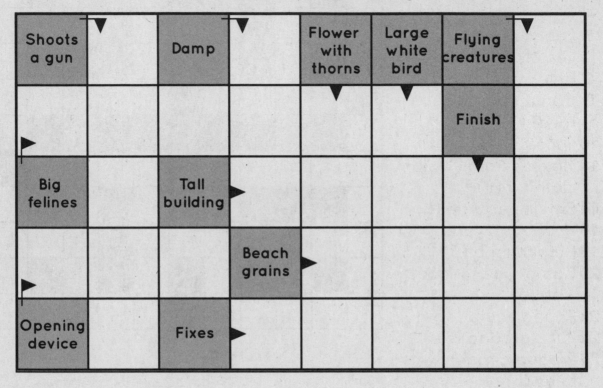

102
X-word

You will find out a heavy material if you write the five-letter answers to the clues in the cross (they all end with the red letter E). Then read the letters in the gray squares to reveal the answer.

1 Frighten
2 Narrow boat with a paddle
3 Move your body to music
4 Hissing creature

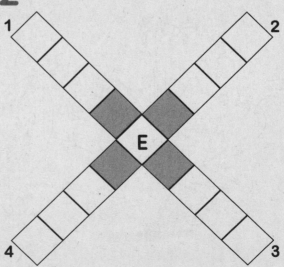

ACROSS

5 Formal school dance (4)

6 The ____ Duckling, story (4)

7 Fizzy drink (3)

8 Exotic fruit or New Zealand bird (4)

9 Sound made by a happy cat (4)

10 Tooth doctor (7)

13 Diver's footwear (7)

17 Set of two (4)

18 Very strong wind (4)

19 Fire remains (3)

20 Leather band worn around the waist (4)

21 Sports side (4)

DOWN

1 Railway vehicle (5)

2 Referee (6)

3 Kermit or Miss Piggy, for example (6)

4 Flower-seller (7)

11 Short sleep (3)

12 Less dirty (7)

14 Sea robber (6)

15 Henry the ____, king who had six wives (6)

16 Cry like a sheep (5)

104
Spiral Puzzle

Fit the answers into the grid – the last letter of one answer is the first of the next. Then, write the letters in the shaded circles in the squares below to spell out the answer to this joke: **Where do ghosts go for a swim?**

1 Not moving (5)
2 Giggle (5)
3 Highest part of the body (4)
4 Items rolled in a game (4)
5 School test (4)
6 Awards won at the Olympics (6)
7 Meal made of lettuce, tomato, etc (5)
8 Song for two people (4)
9 Part of a dog that wags! (4)

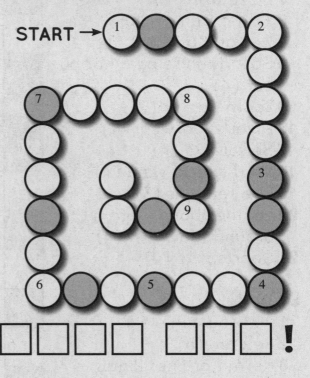

Ghosts swim in ☐☐☐ ☐☐☐☐ ☐☐☐ **!**

105
Letter Play

Try to work out where each of the three-letter words in the list fit into the grid. If you do it correctly the top and bottom horizontal lines of the grid will have one six-letter word and the middle line will have two.

ANT   MED
DAM   PED
LAR   TEN
LIS

		ANT

Picture This

Write the name of each item pictured into the grid, and the circled letters will spell out what kind of boat this captain is the skipper of.

ACROSS

1 Breakfast meat (5)
4 Slow-moving mollusk with a spiral shell (5)
7 Spider's construction (3)
8 Frozen water (3)
9 Item in an auction (3)
10 Uncommon (4)
11 Last match in a competition (5)
14 Difficult to climb (5)
16 Board for carrying dishes (4)
18 Painting, drawing, etc. (3)
20 One of five on a foot (3)
21 Opposite of 'start' (3)
22 Distance from the surface to the bottom (5)
23 Name of a book or film (5)

DOWN

1 Dog's food or water dish (4)
2 Leafy green vegetable (7)
3 Loud sound (5)
4 Ledge fixed to a wall (5)
5 Every single one (3)
6 Tiny, small (6)
12 Closest (7)
13 Area surrounded by water (6)
15 Throw a baseball (5)
16 Special pleasure (5)
17 Lazy (4)
19 Piece of advice (3)

108
Cartoon Crossword

To fill in the blank crossword grid, take the first letter of each pictured item in the grid. For example, box 1 will have a W inside it as it's the first letter of window.

109
Name Game

Complete the answers to the clues and then read down the letters in the gray squares to spell out an adjective.

CLUES

1 Black and white animal
2 Park seat
3 Cash, coins
4 Cuddly toy bear

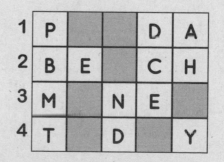

1	P			D	A
2	B	E		C	H
3	M		N	E	
4	T		D		Y

110
Arroword

Write the answers into the squares shown by the arrows.

Flat dish for a dinner ▼		Woman's garment ▼		Young women ▼		Volcanic liquid	Broth
Lion's hair		Train tracks ▶				▼	▼
▶				Rodent ▶			
Chickens		Crack (puzzles) ▶					
▶				Tool for cutting ▶			

111

Letter Code

Write the answers to the clues in the grid. When you've finished, the letters in the gray column will spell out an activity!

CLUES

1 Sink
2 Cash, coins, etc
3 Sweeping brush
4 Animal carrying a jockey
5 Young person
6 Baby rabbit
7 Battle, argument

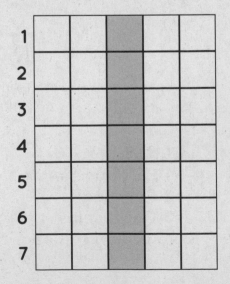

112

ACROSS

1 Smell, perfume (5)
4 Sandy stretch of seashore (5)
7 Daytime snooze (3)
8 Dark-colored fluid used for writing and printing (3)
9 Darkening of the skin in sunlight (3)
10 Very strong wind (4)
11 ____ rehearsal, practice in costume (5)
14 Irritate, pester (5)
16 Opposite of 'quiet' (4)
18 On the ____, punctually (3)
20 Young bear (3)
21 Ice-cream container (3)
22 Opposite of 'left' (5)
23 Opposite of 'little' (5)

DOWN

1 Pale yellow seaside particles (4)
2 Clarify, make clear (7)
3 Group of people headed by a chief (5)
4 ____ beans (5)

5 Perform in a play (3)
6 Trustworthy, truthful (6)
12 Imaginary line round the Earth (7)
13 Climbing device with rungs (6)

15 Pleasure boat with sails (5)
16 Maker's name inside clothing (5)
17 ____ seaman, rank of sailor (4)
19 Style of wrestling for two teams of two (3)

113

ACROSS
2 Space (3)
5 Zero (3)
6 Homer Simpson's wife (5)
9 ___ *Lisa*, famous painting (4)
10 Black bird (4)
12 Beg (5)
14 Fib (3)
15 Father (3)

DOWN
1 Snake's tooth (4)
3 Segment (5)
4 Peter ___, the boy who never grew up (3)
6 Cut the grass (3)
7 Speedy (5)
8 White sea fish (3)
11 Sprinted (3)
13 Let in water (4)

114
Word Ladder

Can you climb down the word ladder from BALL to LINE? Simply change one letter in BALL for the answer to the first clue, then one letter in that answer for the answer to the second clue, and so on.

CLUES
1 Bird's beak
2 Window ledge
3 Natural material
4 Fall gradually,
5 Connect

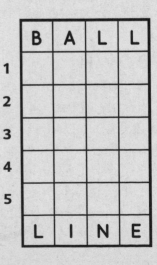

Picture This

Write the name of each item pictured into the grid, and the circled letters will spell out what the boy is hoping to catch.

116

ACROSS
2 Affirmative reply (3)
5 Color of blood (3)
6 Have the same view as someone (5)
9 Small insect often found on a dog (4)
10 A specific day of a month (4)
12 Covered with ashy-white coating (5)
14 What we breathe (3)
15 The first number (3)

DOWN
1 In this place (4)
3 Where plants grow from (5)
4 How old someone is (3)
6 Everything (3)
7 Wireless communication (5)
8 A pig's home (3)
11 Consumed (3)
13 Large vessels for serving tea (4)

117

Write the five answers ending with the letter Y in the grid, so that the letters in the gray squares spell out what a boat has in order to sink.

1 Peanut butter and ____
2 Sweet stuff made by bees
3 Day before tomorrow
4 ____ Way, our galaxy

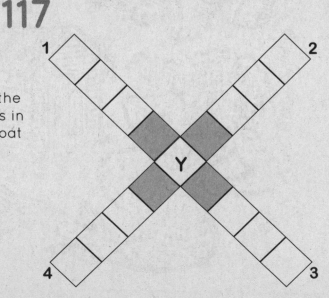

118

ACROSS

1 Japanese wrestling (4)
3 Team of workers on a ship (4)
7 Male sheep (3)
8 Performed in a play (5)
9 Male person (3)
10 Which person? (3)
12 Use a needle and thread (3)
14 Sportsperson, runner (7)
15 Powdery remains of a fire (3)
16 Pixie (3)
18 Honey-making insect (3)
19 Black and white bear-like animal (5)
21 Writing tool (3)
22 Munches, swallows (4)
23 Animal doctors (4)

DOWN

1 Drinking tube (5)
2 Prehistoric elephant (7)
4 Rodent (3)
5 Black ____, venomous spider (5)
6 Steering device on a bike (9)
11 Owns (3)
12 Church spire (7)

13 Long, snake-like fish (3)
15 Orchard fruit such as a Golden Delicious (5)
17 Snake's teeth (5)
20 Almond or cashew (3)

119

Take Five

The answers to these clues are all five-letter words. Enter them into the grid, reading across, and the letters in the diagonal row should spell out a girl's name.

1 Sound made by a frog
2 Not long
3 Person who flies an airplane
4 Christmas song
5 Python or cobra, for example

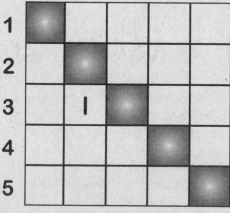

ACROSS
2 Man's best friend (3)
5 A segment of a circle (3)
6 Large marine mammal (5)
9 A silly or stupid person (4)
10 At any time (4)
12 The possessor (5)
14 A double act (3)
15 A Spanish gentleman (3)

DOWN
1 Score in soccer (4)
3 Color of grass (5)
4 Doctor _____, TV program (3)
6 Finished first (3)
7 Not whispered (5)
8 That woman (3)
11 Animal doctor (3)
13 What trees are made of (4)

Word Ladder

Can you climb down the word ladder from MAIN to DOOR? Simply change one letter in MAIN for the answer to the first clue, then one letter in that answer for the answer to the second clue, and so on.

CLUES
1 Reclined
2 Cut of meat
3 Northern seabird
4 Weaving machine
5 Destiny

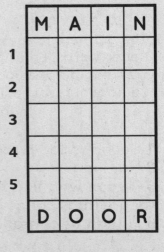

122
Name Game

Dogs are good at fetching things! Complete the grid using the clues, then read down the gray squares to spell out a sort of dog that's good at this.

CLUES
1 Traffic-light color
2 Vehicle that runs on tracks
3 High body temperature
4 Seller of bread

1	G			E	N
2			A		N
3	F			E	R
4	B	A	K		

123
Cartoon Crossword

To fill in the blank crossword grid, take the first letter of each pictured item in the grid. For example, box 1 will have an O inside it as it's the first letter of orange.

ACROSS

2 Speckle, spot (3)
4 Dangerous hooded snake (5)
7 Frozen water (3)
9 Pile (4)
11 Clothes-pins (4)
12 Fire remains (3)
13 Flying toys (5)
15 Mesh for catching fish (3)

DOWN

1 Employment (3)
2 Intelligent sea-mammal (7)
3 One of three identical children (7)
5 Top card (3)
6 Hot drink made with a bag (3)
8 Unborn bird (3)
10 Request (3)
14 Number of years in a decade (3)

125

Name Game

Complete the grid using the clues, then read down the gray squares to spell out a word related to treasures and pirates.

CLUES

1 Group of bees
2 Beach ____, car that can be driven on sand
3 Being from another planet
4 Romantic flowers

1		W	A	R		
2	B					Y
3	A		I		N	
4		O	S	E		

Picture This

Write the name of each item pictured into the grid, and the circled letters will spell out what the boy is waiting for.

Arroword

Write the answers into the squares shown by the arrows.

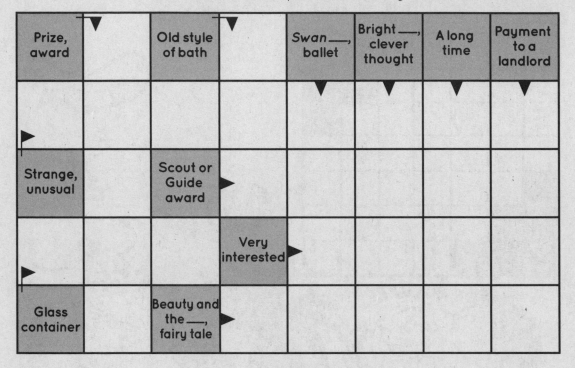

Prize, award	▼	Old style of bath	▼	*Swan* ___, ballet	Bright ___, clever thought	A long time	Payment to a landlord
⚑				▼	▼	▼	▼
Strange, unusual		Scout or Guide award ▶					
⚑			Very interested ▶				
⚑ Glass container		Beauty and the ___, fairy tale ▶					

128

Egg Timer

To answer these clues, remove a letter from the previous answer then rearrange them to get the new answer. When you pass clue 4, you have to do the opposite — adding a letter each time. If you do it correctly, the gray squares will spell out an adjective.

1 Undoes shoelaces
2 Join together
3 Song, melody
4 Mesh used to catch fish
5 ___-deaf, unable to sing or hear music properly
6 Reminders, memos
7 Removed pit from fruit

1 U N T I E S
2
3
4
5
6
7 S T O N E D

129
Star Turn

All the answers to these clues have six letters and end with the letter E. Can you fit the answers in their places in the star? If you manage it correctly you will find that the letters in the gray circles, reading clockwise from the top, spell out the missing word from the joke under the grid.

CLUES

1 King or queen's house
2 Tortoise-like swimming reptile
3 Center
4 Harm or injury
5 Pair of partners
6 Ten years

JOKE:
What do you call a snowman in summer?

A __ __ __ __ __ __!

130
Word Ladder

Can you climb down the ladder from SORE to HEAD? Just change one letter in SORE for the answer to the first clue, then one letter in that answer for the answer to the second clue, and so on.

CLUES

1 Middle of an apple
2 ___ for, look after
3 Animal like a rabbit
4 Difficult
5 Group of cows

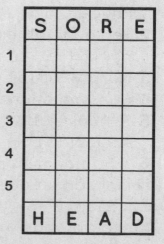

ACROSS

1 Center of the eye (5)
4 Swimming stroke (5)
7 Travel across snow (3)
8 Beaver's construction (3)
9 Towing boat (3)
10 Stare intently (4)
11 Variety of cloth (5)
14 Performance set to music (5)
16 List of information (4)
18 Baby goat (3)
20 Small green vegetable (3)
21 Wise night bird (3)
22 Move to music (5)
23 Foot joint (5)

15 Fruit with a core (5)
16 Stage play (5)
17 Crossword hint (4)
19 Lion's lair (3)

DOWN

1 Fence ___ (4)
2 Personal rather than public (7)
3 Narrow sill (5)
4 Humped animal (5)
5 School craft subject (3)
6 Traditional story (6)
12 Linked computer system (7)
13 Wet through (6)

132
Code Cracker

In this puzzle, you must decide which letter of the alphabet is represented by each of the numbers from 1 to 26. We have already filled in two words, so you can see that B = 20, A = 9, N = 16, and so on. Begin by repeating these letters in each box where their numbers appear in the diagram. You will then have lots of letters to help you start guessing at likely words in the grid. All the letters of the alphabet will be used, so as you decide what each one is, cross it off at the side of the grid and enter it into the reference grid at the bottom. The completed grid will look like a filled-in crossword.

Left labels: A B C D E F G H I J K L M
Right labels: N O P Q R S T U V W X Y Z

23	6	13	10	18		10		20 B	9 A	16 N	22 G		20	
9		16		9		2	6	6			10	14	9	8
2	4	10	10	25	9	4		25	17	26	26		13	
13		10		17		6	9	25		17		20	10	21
21	6	26	26	6	19			6		25	4	10	18	10
9			10		17	25	10	8		18		9		16
24	9	21	21	26	10		3		11	10	2	10	10	25
	11		22		2	18	5	11	4		18		18	
2	4	10	10	11	10		9		9	16	17	8	9	26
5		14		9		2 C	26 L	17 I	19 P		11			9
1	18	17	26	26		9			10	8	19	26	6	7
1	9	25		9		16	17	25		9		10		10
	15		17	21	10	9		5	16	2	6	12	10	18
23	6	17	16			18	17	20		9		10		10
	18		16	6	11	7		9		24	6	18	26	21

C L I P (row with 2 26 17 19)

Reference grid:

1	2	3	4	5	6	7	8	9	10	11	12	13
	C							A				
14	15	16	17	18	19	20	21	22	23	24	25	26
		N	I		P	B		G				L

133

ACROSS

3 Small termite-like insect (3)
7 Large wooded area (6)
8 Scared (6)
9 Glowing ring above an angel's head (4)
10 Long slippery fish (3)
11 Part of a skeleton (4)
12 Vipers (6)
14 Striped or wavy patterned cat (5)
16 Start (5)
18 Group of geese (6)
20 Dutch red-skinned cheese (4)
22 Not young (3)
23 Large extinct bird (4)
24 Dog's shelter (6)
25 Religious spring festival (6)
26 Have a meal (3)

DOWN

1 Person lacking courage (6)
2 Nil (4)
3 Capital city of Greece (6)
4 Pill (6)
5 Sea creature with pincers (4)
6 Walt ____, Mickey Mouse creator (6)
13 Food item with a yolk (3)
15 Large (3)
16 Heavenly ____, The sun, moon and stars (6)
17 Long piece of pasta (6)
18 Inspector ____, cartoon character (6)
19 Climbing equipment (6)
21 Lion's hair (4)
23 Worktable (4)

Picture This

Write the name of each item pictured into the grid, and the circled letters will spell out what weather is forecast.

135

ACROSS

1 Go to see (a person or place) (5)
4 One of the five senses (5)
7 Not very well (3)
8 ___ team, pair of wrestlers (3)
9 Boat used for guiding ships (3)
10 Bird's beak (4)
11 Prickle on a rose (5)
14 Waste material (5)
16 Letters sent by post (4)
18 Point at a target (3)
20 Common rodent (3)
21 Printing fluid (3)
22 Bald ___, symbol of the USA (5)
23 Easily creased cloth (5)

12 Point of view (7)
13 Break out of jail (6)
15 Money holder (5)
16 Lead or iron, for instance (5)
17 Outer covering of the body (4)
19 Large cup for drinking tea (3)

DOWN

1 Thin line in a leaf (4)
2 Person in the army (7)
3 Whole amount (5)
4 Too close-fitting (5)
5 ___ down, use a chair (3)
6 Motor in a car (6)

Picture This

Write the name of each item pictured into the grid, and the circled letters will spell out the type of pet the girl is hoping to take home.

Creature Feature

Solve the clues and write your answers in the grid. If you do so correctly, the shaded column will spell out a beastly word.

1 Yogi ____, cartoon character
2 Santa's four-legged helper
3 Striped wild cat
4 Humped mammal
5 Nocturnal flying mammal
6 Blind burrowing creature
7 Quadruped with hooves and a mane

Word It Out

Solve the clues and write your answers in the grid. If you do so correctly, the shaded line will reveal something to look forward to.

1 Farmyard birds
2 Young swan
3 Opposite of narrow
4 Queen's headwear
5 Settee
6 Cold season
7 Sport played at Wimbledon
8 Language spoken in Paris
9 Little

139

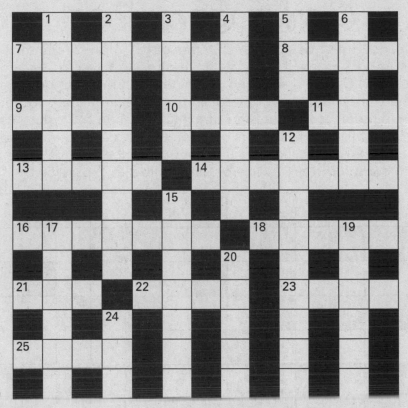

ACROSS

7 Document needed when traveling abroad (8)

8 ____ game, sporting fixture not played at home (4)

9 Mark left by a wound (4)

10 Large town (4)

11 Male child (3)

13 Unable to see (5)

14 Instrument showing north, east, south and west (7)

16 First month of the year (7)

18 Color of coal (5)

21 Twenty-four hours (3)

22 Wise birds (4)

23 Strong wind (4)

25 Capital city of Italy (4)

DOWN

1 Package sent in the post (6)

2 Space traveler (9)

3 Hand-held light (5)

4 Cowboy's hat (7)

5 Jam pot (3)

6 Well-known, like a pop singer or movie star (6)

12 Say sorry (9)

15 Sketching (7)

17 Large river of South America (6)

19 Crunchy salad stick (6)

20 American film award (5)

24 Writing tool (3)

140
Code Cracker

In this puzzle, you must decide which letter of the alphabet is represented by each of the numbers from 1 to 26. We have already filled in two words, so you can see that C = 1, O = 12, A = 21 and so on. Begin by repeating these letters in each box where their numbers appear in the diagram. You will then have lots of letters to help you start guessing at likely words in the grid. All the letters of the alphabet will be used, so as you decide what each one is, cross it off at the side of the grid and enter it into the reference grid at the bottom. The completed grid will look like a filled-in crossword.

10	2	21	15	4		3		4	13	8	2		24	
21		2		13		12	26	26			8	16	12	17
23	21	2	2	4	16	20		26	21	15	4		2	
23		12		16		21	22	4		12		12	21	19
21	2	25	21	20	3			1		6	4	10	16	21
23			1		1 C	12 O	21 A	19 T		4		12		18
4	15 D	8	19	12	16		23		3	17	4	4	6	4
	8 I		12		21	16	4	17	21		7		8	
4	17 N	19	16	21	24		17		10	16	4	21	19	11
13		21		19		3	19	21	16		1			21
4	5	9	21	2		5			4	3	19	4	4	14
17	9	19		21		9	3	4		19		2		3
	4		8	3	2	4		21	1	16	12	10	21	19
25	4	2	2			21	16	1		21		12		4
	17		2	8	1	18		11		24	12	25	4	16

Side labels (left): A B C D E F G H I J K L M
Side labels (right): N O P Q R S T U V W X Y Z

1	2	3	4	5	6	7	8	9	10	11	12	13
C							I				O	

14	15	16	17	18	19	20	21	22	23	24	25	26
	D		N		T		A					

141

ACROSS

1 Opposite of small (3)
3 Walt Disney cartoon fawn (5)
6 Huge mass of snow that hurtles down a mountain (9)
7 Frozen rain (4)
8 Builder of the ark (4)
11 Space traveler (9)
12 Third month (5)
13 Finish (3)

DOWN

1 Sandy area on the coast (5)
2 Fighter in the Roman arena (9)
3 Grizzly or polar animal (4)
4 High-speed cooker (9)
5 Frozen water (3)
9 Loathed, disliked intensely (5)
10 Fluttering insect attracted to light (4)
11 Upper limb (3)

142

Cartoon Crossword

To fill in the blank crossword grid, take the first letter of each pictured item in the grid. For example, box 1 will have a G inside it as it's the first letter of ghost.

143

ACROSS

7 Mother or father (6)
8 Hard hat (6)
9 Primate (3)
10 Turquoise or navy color (4)
11 Magician's stick (4)
12 High-pitched bark (3)
14 Not stale (5)
17 *Beauty and the ___*, fairy tale (5)
19 Type of leaf shown on
    Canada's flag (5)
20 Board-game involving pawns,
    knights, and rooks (5)
22 Grass color (5)
24 Spider's trap (3)
26 Hen's produce (4)
28 Male children (4)
29 Part of a fish (3)
30 Sixty seconds (6)
31 Wild cards in a pack (6)

DOWN

1 Popeye's profession (6)
2 In this place (4)
3 Rome's country (5)
4 Inexpensive (5)
5 Crab's leg (4)
6 Game played with rackets and
    a net (6)
13 Juicy fruit with seeds (5)
15 Seeing organ (3)
16 Initials before a British ship's
    name (3)
17 Plead (3)
18 Exist (3)
21 Harry Potter's giant friend (6)
23 Donkey friend of Winnie-the-Pooh (6)
24 Cookie eaten with ice cream (5)
25 Guitar-like instrument (5)
27 Liquid food (4)
28 Cook in the oven (4)

144

Code Cracker

In this puzzle, you must decide which letter of the alphabet is represented by each of the numbers from 1 to 26. We have already filled in two words, so you can see that I = 1, M = 10, and A = 8. Begin by repeating these letters in each box where their numbers appear in the diagram. You will then have lots of letters to help you start guessing at likely words in the grid. All the letters of the alphabet will be used, so as you decide what each one is, cross it off at the side of the grid and enter it into the reference grid at the bottom. The completed grid will look like a filled-in crossword.

26	13	8	14	22	■	9	■	6	22	20	11	■	6	■
8	■	19	■	1	■	8	22	22	■	■	24	8	19	13
12	13	22	1	2	13	14	■	13	15	24	20	■	20	■
22	■	8	■	1	■	3	1	12	■	13	■	10	20	26
20	16	6	1 I	12	13	■	■	18	■	12	11	13	22	22
15	■	■	10 M	■	2	20	19	13	■	18	■	16	■	8
3	8	14	8 A	19	13	■	14	■	6	13	21	7	1	16
■	18	■	18 G	■	16	13	1	18	24	■	7	■	15	■
12	13	19	13 E	15	19	■	9	■	20 O	26 P	13 E	16 N	13 E	14 R
8	■	13	■	20	■	19	13	8	14	■	6	■	■	8
19	20	4	1	15	■	11	■	■	13	16	19	14	8	26
13	8	19	■	20	■	13	22	23	■	1	■	20	■	1
■	6	■	5	8	1	22	■	8	16	16	20	17	13	12
6	1	25	13	■	■	2	8	16	■	19	■	8	■	22
■	6	■	19	8	3	13	■	18	■	24	1	22	22	17

A B C D E F G H I J K L M

N O P Q R S T U V W X Y Z

1	2	3	4	5	6	7	8	9	10	11	12	13
I							A		M			E
14	**15**	**16**	**17**	**18**	**19**	**20**	**21**	**22**	**23**	**24**	**25**	**26**
R		N		G		O						P

Pyramid

As you answer these clues, you'll see that each answer contains the same letters as the previous answer, plus an extra letter. So, TAP, PART and STRAP could be consecutive answers in a pyramid. Can you complete this one?

1 First letter of the alphabet
2 Meaning of the @ symbol in website addresses
3 Took a chair
4 Final
5 No longer fresh
6 Fortress
7 Schoolbag

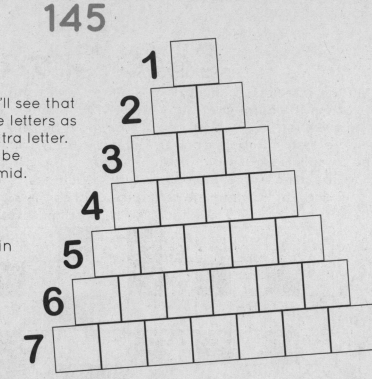

Build A Word

Decide what the answers are to these two sets of clues, and fit them into their respective grids. When you have done so, put together the circled letters from the two grids to spell out one of Bart Simpson's prized possessions.

1 The first day of the week
2 Peel, outer layer
3 Long, thin reptile
4 Closes
5 Frighten

A Color of coal
B Dogs love to chew these
C Water transport
D Facial hair
E Uninterested, fed up

147

ACROSS
3 Large cup (3)
7 Long yellow fruit (6)
8 Forever (6)
9 Injure with a knife (4)
10 Swine (3)
11 Strong wind (4)
12 Flee from danger (6)
14 School tests (5)
16 Part of a flower (5)
18 Heavy hammer (6)
20 Press clothes to remove creases (4)
22 Function, purpose (3)
23 Snake's tooth (4)
24 Grab roughly (6)
25 Hey ___, cartoon (6)
26 Toothed cutting tool (3)

DOWN
1 Prickly desert plant (6)
2 Baby sheep (4)
3 Black and white bird (6)
4 Group of geese (6)
5 Small branch (4)
6 Goes by bike (6)
13 Small black or red insect (3)
15 Chopping tool (3)
16 Mother or father (6)
17 Giggles, snickers (6)
18 Up-and-down playground ride (6)
19 Mild, kind (6)
21 Quick letter (4)
23 Steering organs of a fish (4)

148
Code Cracker

In this puzzle, you must decide which letter of the alphabet is represented by each of the numbers from 1 to 26. We have already filled in two words, so you can see that B = 24, A = 11, C = 21 and so on. Begin by repeating these letters in each box where their numbers appear in the diagram. You will then have lots of letters to help you start guessing at likely words in the grid. All the letters of the alphabet will be used, so as you decide what each one is, cross it off at the side of the grid and enter it into the reference grid at the bottom. The completed grid will look like a filled-in crossword.

Left side labels: A B C D E F G H I J K L M

Right side labels: N O P Q R S T U V W X Y Z

16	11	18		6	10	6		13	17	11	3	3	4	23
3		10		3		17		17		6		11		1
4	12	5	23	11	10	18		11	10	25		10	14	19
4				25		2		21		10		23		11
15	4	24	3	11		11	3	20		7	1	9	4	23
4		11				3					11			7
3	1	7	1	3		4	24	24		22	26	19	23	19
				17		4		4		1				
24 B	11 A	21 C		18 O		22 N	4	11		24	11	3	1	18
4		1						17				11		11
23	10	25	10	7		8	4	7		4	10	2	26	7
1		5		26		4		10		12				17
14	10	11		4	4	23		16	23	10	5	5	4	3
4		22		10		23		17		22		4		11
6	4	22	7	3	1	19		23 L	1 O	7 T		11	23	23

1 O	2	3	4	5	6	7 T	8	9	10	11 A	12	13
14	15	16	17	18 N	19	20	21 C	22	23 L	24 B	25	26

149

ACROSS

7 Male goose (6)
8 ___ Twist, Dickens' character (6)
9 Unwell (3)
10 End of a prayer (4)
11 Lion's long hair (4)
12 Produce eggs (3)
14 Light quick meal (5)
17 Religious book (5)
19 House built of ice (5)
20 Use money (5)
22 Openings in fences (5)
24 America (initials) (3)
26 Scuttling shellfish (4)
28 Massive (4)
29 Female rabbit (3)
30 Glass container for liquid (6)
31 Thirty times three (6)

DOWN

1 Gotham City superhero (6)
2 Garden in the Bible (4)
3 Tool for making holes (5)
4 Prickly plant with red berries (5)
5 Movie (4)
6 Dog's shelter (6)
13 Book of maps (5)
15 Number of years reached (3)
16 Young goat (3)
17 Marshy ground (3)
18 Baseball equipment (3)
21 Colorful talking bird (6)
23 Twenty times four (6)
24 Cow's milk bag (5)
25 Secret ___, spy (5)
27 Nibble (4)
28 Body part with fingers (4)

Name Game

Complete the answers to the clues and then read down the letters in the white squares to spell out the name of a tree that produces sweet edible nuts.

CLUES
1 Squash
2 Item of girls' clothing
3 Elephant's nose
4 Silent

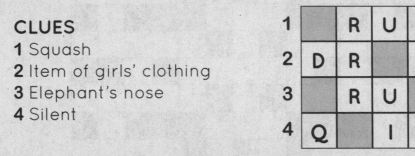

151

Cartoon Crossword

To fill in the blank crossword grid, take the first letter of each pictured item in the grid. For example, box 1 will have a Y inside it as it's the first letter of yo-yo.

Animal Antics

In this puzzle, you have to match each animal with its correct noise. For example in number 1, the cow should be saying MOO! So, what you have to do, is find the moo, write it in the grid, then note down the G from the bottom right of the moo picture. If you do this correctly, you should spell out the name of an animal reading down the right-hand side of the grid.

ACROSS

5 ____ -hoop, round toy (4)
6 Sixty minutes (4)
7 Book of photographs (5)
8 Cunning, underhand (3)
10 Place where planes land and take off (7)
11 Sob (3)
12 Mass of wasps (5)
15 Large town (4)
16 Financial building (4)

DOWN

1 Opposite of empty (4)
2 First month (7)
3 Timid (3)
4 Item fired from a gun (6)
9 Spiders' traps (7)
10 Scared (6)
13 The doorbell ___ (4)
14 Place where people work out (3)

Picture Code

The first answer in each row ends in the gray square, and the second answer starts in the gray square. When you've answered all the clues, the letters in the gray column will spell out what pirates search for.

CLUES

1 Jacket • Chat, speak
2 Opposite of 'rich' • Look at a book
3 Adore • Not odd
4 Jumping insect • Uncle's wife
5 Places to sleep • Chair
6 List of food in a restaurant • Opposite of 'pretty'
7 Sixty minutes • Running competition
8 Bee's home • Wicked

155

ACROSS

3 Public transport vehicle (3)
7 Glass container (6)
8 Photographer's equipment (6)
9 Wintry weather (4)
10 Man's neckwear (3)
11 Beach grains (4)
12 Horse's shelter (6)
14 Third month (5)
16 Vacation accommodation (5)
18 Arm joints (6)
20 Last word of a prayer (4)
22 Geographical chart (3)
23 Wet weather (4)
24 Autumn or winter, for example (6)
25 Lump of gold (6)
26 Unhappy (3)

DOWN

1 Easter hat (6)
2 Casserole, soup (4)
3 Hard-backed insect (6)
4 Frightened yell (6)
5 Large, flightless birds (4)
6 From Paris, perhaps (6)
13 Nocturnal flying mammal (3)
15 Chest bone (3)
16 Tool for banging in nails (6)
17 Yellow sour fruits (6)
18 Grow bigger (6)
19 Cafe worker (6)
21 Bird's home (4)
23 Anger (4)

156
Code Cracker

In this puzzle, you must decide which letter of the alphabet is represented by each of the numbers from 1 to 26. We have already filled in two words, so you can see that S = 4, T = 13, A = 11 and so on. Begin by repeating these letters in each box where their numbers appear in the diagram. You will then have lots of letters to help you start guessing at likely words in the grid. All the letters of the alphabet will be used, so as you decide what each one is, cross it off at the side of the grid and enter it into the reference grid at the bottom. The completed grid will look like a filled-in crossword.

Left side: A B C D E F G H I J K L M
Right side: N O P Q R S T U V W X Y Z

1	2	3	4	1	■	5	■	6	3	3	7	■	8	■
9	■	5	■	10	■	11	8	9	■	■	2	7	3	12
4	9	13	14	11	8	1	■	2	13	9	15	■	16	■
13	■	9	■	17	■	9	18	18	■	17	■	11	18	9
16	19	10	10	9	16	■	6	■	9	20	19	2	21	
9	■	■	19	■	19	10	2	13	■	10	■	10	■	2
12	9	10	13	2	12	■	7	■	4(S)	13(T)	11(A)	13(T)	2(I)	8(C)
■	9	■	13	■	9	22	9	8	13	■	8	■	8	■
21	12	11	23	9	16	■	11	■	11	10	13	6	9	15
11	■	16	■	24	■	5	12	11	13	■	3	■	■	2
8	3	15	15	11	■	11	■	■	9	11	16	25	2	18
13	16	23	■	8	■	16	3	7	■	■	■	11	■	16
■	14	■	11(A)	13(T)	3(O)	15(M)	■	16	9	21	12	2	8	11
26	2	10	8	■	■	9	15	19	■	11	■	4	■	13
■	13	■	13	3	19	16	■	18	■	12	■	13	■	9

Reference grid:

1	2	3	4	5	6	7	8	9	10	11	12	13
I	O	S					C			A		T

14	15	16	17	18	19	20	21	22	23	24	25	26
	M											

ACROSS

5 Close by (4)
6 Center of an apple (4)
7 Glide on 3 down (5)
8 Finish (3)
10 Fast-moving big cat (7)
11 Long-legged running bird (3)
12 Long wooden seat (5)
15 Instrument played with sticks (4)
16 Large pond (4)

DOWN

1 Bird's bill (4)
2 Close male relation (7)
3 Frozen water (3)
4 Arm of a tree (6)
9 Church spire (7)
10 Photographer's equipment (6)
13 Sponge or angel food, for example (4)
14 A mischievous child (3)

158

Word Ladder

Can you climb down the word ladder from WET to DRY? Simply change one letter in WET for the answer to the first clue, then one letter in that answer for the answer to the second clue, and so on.

CLUES

1 Animal kept at home
2 Pet a dog's head
3 Took a chair
4 Speak
5 Opposite of 'night'

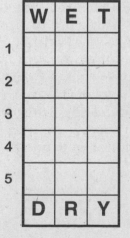

W	E	T
1		
2		
3		
4		
5		
D	R	Y

159

ACROSS
1 Opposite of below (5)
4 Baby lion (3)
6 Small, sweet orange (9)
7 Sunbeams (4)
9 Chef (4)
11 Large group of musicians (9)
13 Mesh for catching fish (3)
14 Begin (5)

DOWN
1 Time between morning and evening (9)
2 Possess, have (3)
3 Seeing organs (4)
4 Capital of Egypt (5)
5 First meal of the day (9)
8 Sailing boat (5)
10 Hive-dwellers (4)
12 Hot drink made with a bag (3)

160

Cartoon Crossword

To fill in the blank crossword grid, take the first letter of each pictured item in the grid. For example, box 1 will have a T inside it as it's the first letter of triangle.

161

ACROSS

1 Coral barrier (4)
3 Gag, funny story (4)
7 Small green pod vegetable (3)
8 Foot joint (5)
9 Farm animal (3)
10 Take a chair (3)
12 Undercover agent (3)
14 Weather conditions (7)
15 Lock opener (3)
16 Small black insect (3)
18 Military conflict (3)
19 Bird of prey (5)
21 Foot digit (3)
22 Young sheep (4)
23 Warmth (4)

DOWN

1 Thick corded strings (5)
2 Precisely (7)
4 Acorn tree (3)
5 Foe (5)
6 Machine for cutting the grass (9)
11 Frozen water (3)
12 Take by surprise (7)
13 Writing tool (3)
15 Rest on bended legs (5)
17 Chirp of a small bird (5)
20 Chewy sweet (3)

162

ACROSS

7 Male parent (6)
8 Team game played with sticks (6)
9 Exist (3)
10 Applaud (4)
11 Wet weather (4)
12 Pixie (3)
14 Main stem of a plant (5)
17 Board-game played with pawns, knights, and rooks (5)
19 Snow house (5)
20 Use money (5)
22 Finger, toe, or number (5)
24 Perform in a play (3)
26 Crab's leg (4)
28 Leak water slowly (4)
29 Purpose (3)
30 Place of learning (6)
31 Set of relatives (6)

DOWN

1 Classical dancing (6)
2 Potato ___, snack (4)
3 Courageous (5)
4 Ledge (5)
5 Mark of an old wound (4)
6 Very brainy person (6)
13 Pale shade of purple (5)
15 Highest playing-card (3)
16 Young goat (3)
17 White fish (3)
18 Omelette ingredient (3)
21 Royal residence (6)
23 Hanging piece of frozen water (6)
24 Grown-up (5)
25 Robbery (5)
27 Sheep's fleece (4)
28 Slightly wet (4)

163
Code Cracker

In this puzzle, you must decide which letter of the alphabet is represented by each of the numbers from 1 to 26. We have already filled in two words, so you can see that D =11, A = 18, I = 25 and so on. Begin by repeating these letters in each box where their numbers appear in the diagram. You will then have lots of letters to help you start guessing at likely words in the grid. All the letters of the alphabet will be used, so as you decide what each one is, cross it off at the side of the grid and enter it into the reference grid at the bottom. The completed grid will look like a filled-in crossword.

Left side labels: A B C D E F G H I J K L M

Right side labels: N O P Q R S T U V W X Y Z

21	18	3	■	20	6	8	■	2	24	18	17	15	25	20
18	■	6	■	3	■	3	■	12	■	14	■	4	■	18
20	18	8	8	18	16	2	■	21	2	15	■	25	12	12
7	■	■	■	23	■	18	■	10	■	2	■	12	■	15
11 D	18 A	25 I	17 S	22 Y	■	7	2	22	■	3	18	12	16	2
18	■	24	■	■	■	14	■	■	■	■	■	2	■	2
5	18	24	15	23	■	18	9	2	■	4	2	3	10	12
■	■	■	■	10	■	17	■	18	■	18	■	■	■	■
3	10	11	2	10	■	15	18	3	■	17	18	19	2	11
2	■	5	■	■	■	■	15	■	■	■	18	■	2	
1	6	25	2	15	■	18	17	4	■	20	18	12	18	24
6	■	12	■	2	■	13	■	24	■	3	■	■	■	25
2	12	11	■	26 M	18 A	13 P	■	25	20	2	8	2	3	16
17	■	24	■	13	■	24	■	12	■	18	■	18	■	4
15	4	2	18	15	3	2	■	16	2	26	■	3	10	15

Reference grid:

1	2	3	4	5	6	7	8	9	10	11 D	12	13 P
14	15	16	17 S	18 A	19	20	21	22 Y	23	24	25 I	26 M

164
Picture This

Write the name of each item pictured in the grid and then read down the circled letters to discover what this kitten is called.

ACROSS
1 Swift rabbit-like mammal (4)
3 Head cook (4)
7 Travel on snow (3)
8 Very fast (5)
9 Fib (3)
10 Cutting tool (3)
12 Father (3)
14 Laughs like a witch (7)
15 Pigpen (3)
16 Bashful, timid (3)
18 Large monkey (3)
19 Small lizard-like amphibians (5)
21 Uncooked (3)
22 Hardworking insects (4)
23 Requests (4)

DOWN
1 Flexible watering pipes (5)
2 Train transport system (7)
4 Jump on one leg (3)
5 Lost color, became paler (5)
6 Morning meal (9)
11 Take part in a play (3)
12 Sahara and Gobi, for instance (7)
13 Gray powder left after a fire (3)
15 ____ Claus, Father Christmas (5)
17 Shows tiredness (5)
20 Soaking (3)

Shade It

To find out what this guy is, fit the answers into the grid and read down the shaded column.

CLUES
1 Clear liquid
2 House made of ice
3 Striped horse
4 Grown-up person
5 Opposite of "left"
6 Filthy

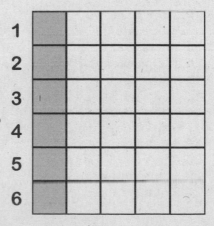

167

ACROSS

7 Santa's transport (6)
8 Person in charge of a newspaper (6)
9 Substance we breathe (3)
10 Having no hair (4)
11 Performed tunefully (4)
12 Instrument to unlock a door (3)
14 Movie award (5)
17 Half of one hundred (5)
19 Fourth month (5)
20 Run away (5)
22 Signs of tiredness (5)
24 Place for exercise (3)
26 Last word of a prayer (4)
28 Tree-trunk covering (4)
29 Upper limb (3)
30 Small earthquake (6)
31 Heavenly ____, The sun, moon and stars (6)

DOWN

1 Noises made by a lamb (6)
2 Feathered creature (4)
3 Soft white rock used for writing (5)
4 Red fruit found on holly (5)
5 Noise made by a snake (4)
6 Easter hat (6)
13 Opposite of late (5)
15 Road vehicle (3)
16 Male sheep (3)
17 Go by air (3)
18 Not many (3)
21 Photograph-taking equipment (6)
23 Hospital workers (6)
24 Person who keeps watch (5)
25 Black ____, deadly African snake (5)
27 Title (4)
28 Unopened flowers (4)

Picture This

Write the name of each item pictured into the grid, and the letters reading diagonally downwards will reveal what is making this boy leap out of the sea.

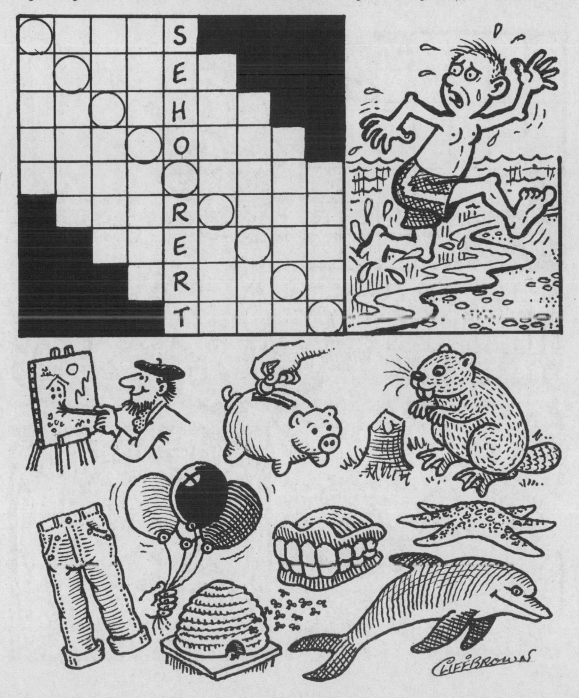

Picture This

Find out what's wrong with this little boy by writing the name of each item pictured into the grid. The answer will read diagonally down the circled letters.

170

ACROSS
7 Hot season (6)
8 Jennifer Aniston's character in Friends (6)
9 On ___, broadcasting (3)
10 In addition (4)
11 Place where savings are kept (4)
12 Opposite of high (3)
14 Book of maps (5)
17 Young women (5)
19 Overhead (5)
20 Body's red fluid (5)
22 Conjuror's art (5)
24 Provided with food (3)
26 Plant stalk (4)
28 Cut with an axe (4)
29 Sticky chewing sweet (3)
30 Hunt (6)
31 Classical dancing (6)

DOWN
1 Missile shot from a gun (6)
2 Pixies (4)
3 Move on hands and knees (5)
4 Missile shot from a bow (5)
5 Crust on a wound (4)
6 Dog's shelter (6)
13 ___ layer, threatened atmospheric layer (5)
15 Zodiac lion (3)
16 Unhappy (3)
17 Precious stone (3)
18 Piece of old cloth (3)
21 One of twenty-six in the alphabet (6)
23 Removed creases from clothes (6)
24 Combat (5)
25 Disney elephant (5)
27 Female horse (4)
28 Young cow (4)

171

ACROSS
1 Speed contest (4)
3 Unwanted plant (4)
7 Animal doctor (3)
8 Large sea (5)
9 Fishes' swimming organ (3)
10 Zero (3)
12 Number of years old (3)
14 Portable light (7)
15 Swiss mountain (3)
16 Wet earth (3)
18 Baby's apron (3)
19 Tool for boring holes (5)
21 Plus, also (3)
22 Waterside grass (4)
23 Really lazy (4)

DOWN
1 Black bird (5)
2 Small entrance in a door for a pet (7)
4 Female sheep (3)
5 Move to music (5)
6 British police officer (9)
11 Unwell (3)
12 What aid workers wear on their arms (7)
13 Large antelope, anagram of GUN (3)
15 Viper (5)
17 Move quickly out of the way (5)
20 Frozen water (3)

Picture This

Decide where each item pictured should be placed in the grid, and if you do so correctly, the circled letters will spell out the woman's profession.

X-Word

The answers to these clues are all five-letter words ending in E, the center letter. Write your answers in the grid starting from the outer squares, then rearrange the letters in the shaded squares to discover a dried fruit.

1 Gaze rudely
2 Vine fruit
3 Operate a car
4 Genetic copy

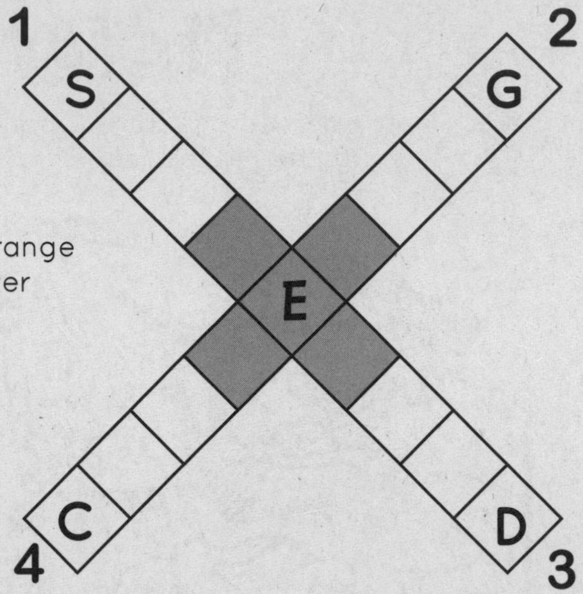

Twofold

Solve this puzzle by choosing one of the two words given in each clue and writing it in the diagram.

ACROSS
1 Draft, drift
6 Agony, ivory
7 Lap, lay
9 Blew, drew
11 Male, move
13 Lie, pie
14 Seas, sway
16 Raps, rats
19 Peg, pug
20 Carve, lodge
21 Nudge, nurse

DOWN
1 Deed, deep
2 Able, ogle
3 Tin, tip
4 Soda, solo
5 Tape, type
8 Ally, awls
10 Roe, row
11 Mare, mere
12 Lag, vat
14 Sock, sulk
15 Ache, acre
17 Aged, agog
18 Sale, salt
19 Pen, pet

175

ACROSS

7 Jumped on one leg (6)
8 Truthful (6)
9 Female rabbit (3)
10 King of the jungle (4)
11 Sports side (4)
12 Crimson (3)
14 Snow house (5)
17 Extra-terrestrial (5)
19 Grown-up (5)
20 Long, pointed weapon (5)
22 Foe (5)
24 Pigpen (3)
26 Creature that scuttles sideways (4)
28 Skeleton part (4)
29 Delivery vehicle (3)
30 Ten-year period (6)
31 Japanese martial art (6)

DOWN

1 Dull, tedious (6)
2 Opposite of shut (4)
3 Viper (5)
4 In front (5)
5 Small fly (4)
6 Flee (6)
13 Explode, like a volcano (5)
15 Fib (3)
16 Paddle (3)
17 Devoured (3)
18 Frozen water (3)
21 Package (6)
23 One sixtieth of an hour (6)
24 Rescues (5)
25 Pulls hard (5)
27 Bird's bill (4)
28 Naked (4)

Code Cracker

In this puzzle, you must decide which letter of the alphabet is represented by each of the numbers from 1 to 26. We have already filled in two words, so you can see that O = 4, Z = 11, N = 16 and E = 14. Begin by repeating these letters in each box where their numbers appear in the diagram. You will then have lots of letters to help you start guessing at likely words in the grid. All the letters of the alphabet will be used, so as you decide what each one is, cross it off at the side of the grid and enter it into the reference grid at the bottom. The completed grid will look like a filled-in crossword.

Left column letters: A B C D E F G H I J K L M
Right column letters: N O P Q R S T U V W X Y Z

25	24	9	24	25	■	12	■	22	24	13	17	■	4	■
14	■	14	■	16	■	24	19	4	■	■	13	16	5	26
15	14	24	15	13	5	25	■	15	17	24	6	■	14	■
7	■	15	■	12	■	14	24	7	■	10	■	12	24	7
20	4	7	7	14	20	■	■	17	■	4 O	11 Z	4 O	16 N	14 E
14	■	■	26	■	26	4	6	14	■	21	■	4	■	24
17	23	2	23	20	9	■	24	■	17	14	24	8	14	20
■	15	■	1	■	1	24	16	19	4	■	8	■	20	■
6	14	10	10	17 L	14	■	8	■	5	24	1	14	20	24
24	■	4	■	14 E	■	8	24	7	24	■	13	■	■	6
19	14	16	13	14 E	■	14	■	■	17	14	7	7	14	20
14	21	14	■	5 C	■	14	16	8	■	18	■	13	■	13
■	14	■	15	26 H	13	6	■	24	18	23	24	7	13	5
19	16	24	7	■	■	14	17	12	■	13	■	17	■	4
■	7	■	9	24	3	16	■	7	■	6	17	14	24	7

Reference grid:

1	2	3	4	5	6	7	8	9	10	11	12	13
			O	C						Z		

14	15	16	17	18	19	20	21	22	23	24	25	26
E		N	L									H

Solutions

1
```
SEE HUT
SUIT  ROUT
TRACTOR
STRETCH
MUG WET
```

2
```
DYE ANT
DAB
DUG OUT
EMU
YES TAR
```

3
```
LONDON ACORNS
GEM
HULA   DAHL
YES
DENIM  IVORY
ALBUM
SALAD  PANDA
OWL
BRIM   HUGE
TEN
ESCAPE ANSWER
```

4
```
BEACH BRASS
ASH AID ROD
TEST EASEL
EVENT SOLO
POT AGE NOD
EXACT PIECE
```

5
```
HOP PAW
LANTERN
SNAIL
STUDENT
SEA TAP
```

6
```
APRIL
ROBOT
LATIN
```

7
```
MUSHROOM
GAP CARGO
CARD STOP
ANKLE USE
SYLLABLE
```

8
```
MANE
AREA
NEAR
EARS
```

9
```
COCOA PILOT
ROB GUN DEN
RAKE CRANE
OPERA HARD
GET RAT BEE
EAGLE HOTEL
```

10
```
HIVE
FAIRY
MALLET
PELICAN
COWBOY
SCOUT
FOOT
```
The fish is a **HALIBUT**

11
```
FISH HENS
AXE UDDER
ROT
TUB SON
SEAGULL
PET ADD
ARM
CHEAP MEN
STEM EDAM
```

12
```
PRECARIOUS
POISE   SWAY
SHAKE
EQUILIBRIUM
LURCH
TREMBLE SLIP
COMPOSURE
```

When you go surfing you might need a **WETSUIT.**

13
```
JEWEL M QUIZ B
A A E EMU OVAL
CLIMATE ALSO S
K S S TAR A PIG
POTATO R FALSE
O N CITY E A N
TANGLE A ORANGE
G E ALLOW B E
GOBLIN O NOODLE
A A D KNEE U
TASTE A ROTTEN
ELK A RUN X E
T FLEA ECLIPSE
HERE TAX I E
R EDGE T PLEAT
```

14
```
TEA PAD
LETTERS
MODEL
ELASTIC
POT DUE
```

15

1 Parrot
2 Even
3 Tomato
4 East
5 Rabbit
6 Panda
7 Ajar
8 Neighbors.
The book is **PETER PAN** by **J M BARRIE.**

16

```
FOOT
PIXIE
CASTLE
KEYHOLE
 STAIRS
   RHINO
   FROG
```

Fred has gone **FISHING**

17

```
      A
     OFF
  G  T  P
  BREEZES
  LIE R DAY
  BEANBAG
    N O L
    BOX
      N
```

18

1 Green 2 Chalk 3 Clock 4 Loose
5 Light: **GHOST**

19

```
   D  E C C A B
KANGAROO  CORE
N G O C E    R
KISS WOOL BEN
S  H N N S Z
THIEF BUTCHER
     L  P  T  H
ANTLERS COATS
  A  S O C O A
FRY STAR LILY
R  F E U B K
FOAL COMPOSER
W  Y T  B Y D
```

20

```
VISIT  SWAMP
A H H  T I O
SEA OAR DEN
E M R A   I
 OPEN PASTE
I O    U S
GROUP SONG
N  I P R B
OUT LIE ICE
R  O N S A
EVENT DREAM
```

21

MIS	LAY	OUT
HIT	MAN	AGE

22

```
   B A E C L B
LONDON ANIMAL
 T A G M M M
STEM ICE BABE
 L N N R O
DECADE AMAZON
   L     R
ADULTS RECIPE
 A  P E  I
KNEE LAP CALF
 C A A A O L
FERRIS IGLOOS
 R N H R D W
```

23

```
CLAW
FRUIT
SPIDER
MAMMOTH
 SEESAW
 IGLOO
  MOON
```

The color the artist needs is **CRIMSON**

24

```
ICE   C K
 GREASE
LEG  BOYS
 SPY L E
A L NOTE
S CAKE I
SHUT WAGE
 BEE  PEN
NESS  HERD
```

25

```
BLACK
E N M
A C M
CHINA
H E G
 N I
ATTIC
```

26

1 WORE
2 WIRE
3 FIRE
4 FIRM

27

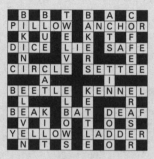
```
 B B T B A C
PILLOW ANCHOR
K U E K T F
DICE LIE SAFE
N V R E E
CIRCLE SETTEE
 A I
BEETLE KENNEL
 L L E R
BEAK BAT DEAF
V I O T O S
YELLOW LADDER
 N T S E O R
```

28

```
SUMO  CREW
T  A H A  I
RAM ACTED
A  MAN  O
WHO D SEW
 ATHLETE
ASH E ELF
P   BEE AN
PANDA PEN G
L  U R L G
EATS VETS
```

29

```
   B
  GEM
 BONES
B S AID
COAL SPIN
ALI L G
 ENTER
 GAS N
```

30

1 Panda 2 Pedal 3 Jerry 4 Quack
5 Watch: **PERCH**

31

```
FLEET  ATTIC
I X W  S A A
NAP  INK  PAN
D   L C E   D
ROPE   DRILL
A   D     C E
DRESS  WEED
U   I A B T
LAW  LOG  EYE
T H L   O R S
STORY  NIGHT
```

32

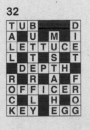

```
TUB      D
A  U  M  I
LETTUCE  T
L L T S T
 DEPTH
R R A F
OFFICER
C   L O
KEY   EGG
```

33

1 Saddle
2 Paris
3 Acorn
4 Rubber
5 Kettle
6 London
7 Eagle
8 Raisin

The hidden word is **SPARKLER**.

34

```
SHOE
GHOST
VIOLIN
SNOWMAN
SNEEZE
 SHARK
 PONY
```

The weather is going to be
SHOWERY

35

```
D B D   G W J
VOLUME  AVENUE
U R V   R E I
OBEY  ILL  KICK
L   L     E E
NEEDLE  CAMERA
O         E
STICKS  NOTICE
O   T   O
PUMA  ABC  TERM
C R R  E W N
PARENT  SPIDER
N A S  T N R
```

36

```
TOAST  ROBIN
I I I  A A A
CAR  ROD  GET
K P E  A   I
 MOSS  RODEO
D R    O   N
EXTRA  SALT
F   W H P O
ELF  AGE  HOP
A A R L I E
TIRED  LINEN
```

37

```
    V  S  A  P  O  L
GALLOP  RABBIT
  N  E  ROO  E  Z
BIRD  I  N  YEAR
  S     LEG  R
CHINA  A  BLADE
     C  CURVE  I
BLEAT  T  DARTS
  A     WHO     A
FULL  A  W  SETT
  G  E  FAN  H  T
CHEESE  EDITOR
  S  K  R  D  P  O
```

38

```
VENOM  E  AREA  Q
A  O  O  CAR   CLUB
MAMMOTH  RAFT  I
P  A  S  OWE  A  FLY
INDEED   S  BRUTE
R  X  REST  L  S  A
ESCAPE  A  METEOR
H  C  AGILE  A  N
SYSTEM  N  ROBBER
I  T  A  STAG  L  I
CHAIR  E  ELEVEN
KEY  T  TEA  O  E  G
R  SHUT  JOURNAL
DOZE  ERASURE
N  WEAR  R  EJECT
```

39

```
   C
  YES
 E LAP
SMALL H
FOUR AMEN
 B RIDER
 COT  W
 WET
  M
```

40

Plastic, Freedom,
Manager, Another,
Weather, Grilled,
Mineral
SEATTLE

41

```
COCK
DRESS
SPIDER
BUTCHER
 DONKEY
  ANGEL
   FEET
```

The sport is **CRICKET**

42

```
     D
    ROD
 P  DAD
BACON  E
HOWL  CENT
X  AHEAD
TWO   R
 SUN
  R
```

43

1 Chess 2 Zebra 3 Uncle 4 Quill
5 Ideas 6 Thief 7 Laugh 8 Jumbo
9 White 10 Scare 11 River:
CAULIFLOWER

44

```
T B P  S M P
SAMUEL  POISON
II G F  O T N
EGGS  AGO  TICK
H   S  K   H
STATUE  YELLOW
  A       A
DWARFS  COSTAR
I   U L   B
ASIA  PRO  WARP
D R P  U O U
POLICE  DROOPY
M D R  Y D T
```

45

```
B K S   C S A
PEANUT EATING
A  E  R L A T
CUBE  EEL  BALD
T     E  E A  E
CYGNET   RETURN
   O        O
CLOWNS   HAMMER
A   A    E    A
HUGE TEA  COST
G  N  U  R  U I
SHIVER  TABLET
S  Y  N   S S R
```

46

```
      P
     ROT
 P   OIL
HEART   A
FOAL  LEND
 P  BLEAT
  CUE   R
   MEW
    K
```

47

```
OTHER
VE OL  L
NOISE
S  DA VE
LAYER
```

48

```
 F  C  A B
FLEA  ROLL
A  EAR  E
ASKS  OKAY
K  A  W T
  CROSSES
A  A   A D
BLANKET
A  E  A P
EDGE  SAIL
D  DOT  X
GILL  EVIL
N  E  R E
```

49

```
SATIN  FEE
C  O  USA  A
RAW  TUNES
O   P  N   I
OWNED  SEE
GONE   K  S
END  WAIST
```

50

```
CRICKETS
STICKER
STRIKE
SKIRT
RISK
SKI
SINK
KINGS
ASKING
SKATING
STACKING
```

51

```
QUAKE B JOKE  A
U B A AXE  WITH
AMONGST SIZE  T
R V L HOT E TIC
TEEPEE  EMBRACE
E A AJAR R X D
RUNNER B NATIVE
 S D TABLE R A
DETACH O IGUANA
E  H STAG S E
ASSAULT  HATTER
FAT N URN L W O
 L SKID ILLNESS
LAVA  INN E E O
D DODO  E YODEL
```

52

```
MASK
ZEBRA
BEAVER
FEATHER
 TRIPOD
 FRUIT
 CAKE
```

The chef is going to make a
MEAT PIE

53

```
 I C C  C B I
ANCHOR  ORANGE
 S E A  B L N
DEAF DEW  DRIP
 C  L  E  T T
STABLE  BIDDER
   A       I
DOCTOR  AUGUST
 R  A  N  U
OPEN BIT  BOMB
 H E B  L O M
SAFARI  ECLAIR
 N T T  R D T
```

54

```
   K
   BIB
  C WAG
MAGIC  J
BATH OVAL
 P OWNER
   USE T
   TAP
    K
```

55

Big, Funny, Naughty, Boomerang, Electricity, Edinburgh, Thirsty, Smell, Sad: **GINGERBREAD**

56

```
ARROWS  BAMBOO
C R I S  A W O U
R O S A W I T
O W HONEY L L L
SALT  T A  FLEA
 S  H A L  W
 FLOCK  SPADE
A R  C  S Y
MOAN  A  KITE
A C MYRRH C L
Z T I O A  E
O  C L  L  L
NEPHEW  DONALD
```

57

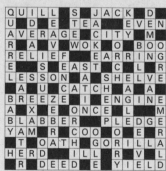

```
QUILL S JACK  D
U D E TEA  EVEN
AVERAGE CITY  M
R A V WOK O BOO
RELIEF  EARRING
E  S EAST C L R
LESSON A SHELVE
A  U CATCH A A
BREEZE I ENGINE
A X E ONCE L M
BLABBER  PLEDGE
YAM R COO  E R
T OATH GORILLA
HERD  ILL R V L
R DEED  E YIELD
```

58

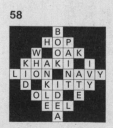

```
    B
   HOP
  W OAK
KHAKI  I
LION NAVY
 D KITTY
  OLD E
  EEL
   A
```

59

1 Roof 2 Adam 3 Mini 4 Robs 5 Ring
6 Room 7 Solo 8 Undo 9 Thin
10 Down: **FAIRGROUND**

60

61

62

The boy is going to go
SURFING

63

64

65

WARM, WORM, FORM, FORT,
FOOT, FOOL, COOL.

66

```
T R A I T   F I T N E S S
A   R   H   A   E   M   I
C I R C U I T   E Q U I P
K   O   M   N   P   P
L E G I B L E   A P P L E
E   A   X   G   R   D
  I N T E R P R E T E R
W   C   E   C   O
A R E A S   L A R G E L Y
N   T   A   D   S
D R A P E   E N T R E A T
E   I   R   V   I N   E
R O M A N C E   O U T E R
```

67

```
B   U   B   C   B   C
D A G G E R   R A I S I N
T   L   U   A   R   R
S T A Y   N E T   D U C K
E   Z   E       U
B R E E Z E   R A D I S H
    L       L       A
P U F F I N   B O D I E S
M   E       O       D
S P I N   A C T   F O I L
I   A       O       T
T R A V E L   N A R R O W
E   Y   Y   Y   K   R
```

68

```
J E W E L   L   M Y N A   A
A   I   E   E G O   G A T E
C A P T A I N   D I C E   L
K   E   V   S K I   O   F A T
D A R K E N   F U R N I S H
A   H   U G L Y   G   Z   U
W I Z A R D   A   Z I G Z A G
C   K   G O R S E   R   R
D E F I N E   G   B L E A C H
E   U   O   S E E R   A   O
A C R O B A T   A C T I O N
F I Y   I   A Y F   A   E
  O   S E E P   D E P R E S S
Q U I T   L E G   E   A T
  D   Y O K E   E   R A L L Y
```

69

Premier, Disease, Element,
Chapter, Fashion, Patient, Message
MEMPHIS

70

1 Seven 2 Even 3 House 4 Hose
5 Sport 6 Pots 7 froze 8 Zero
9 Bleat 10 Late 11 Roast 12 Star
13 Spain 14 Spin 15 Rapid 16 Paid
17 Drake 18 Rake: **SURFBOARD**

71

72

The girl is searching for a
COWSLIP

73

74

Caribbean, Astronaut, Satisfied,
Breathing, Halloween, Sprinkles
The city is **BOSTON.**

75

```
STOOP LIBRARY
W V R I L C A
AWESOME ATTIC
T R B T H
HOSTESS ADAPT
E H O N B S
COMPILATION
C O R I L L
OUTDO DECLINE
S V A T A
MIDGE WEDDING
O I R A E O U
SANDBAG TENSE
```

76

```
JOKED A EASE I
A E R MAD VEST
CABBAGE IDLE S
K A W NIB E PUS
PEBBLE LEAFLET
O U NAME S E A
TABLET O STEADY
G G EXTRA Q I
METEOR T LOUNGE
A O L SOFA A L
ZILLION DILUTE
END V ASS C N M
D ZEST WHISTLE
ZERO C N IN
X OUCH P GREAT
```

77

```
MUD POP
EE R A
ANCIENT
L O S H
BRAIN
S A D S
PATIENT
I E N E
NOD TOW
```

78

```
SUPER
A R
N E M
TASTE
A E A
N L
NOTES
```

79

```
B K G J
TREE IRON
A NIB U
OVEN BARE
E E O N
BLANKET
C R Y
CHICKEN
A A I A
OPEN GALE
T ASH B
YEAR TRUE
R Y Y M
```

80

```
COM BAT HER
MIT TEN DED
```

81

```
TREE
SWEEP
CHERUB
BOWLING
PUFFIN
TEETH
FISH
```

The boy's birthday is on the
TWELFTH

82

```
F T S J S F
BESIDE UNHURT
E M A M O I
OBOE LIP EYES
L E E N
YELLED DECIDE
O O
CLOSET MEDIUM
E E O O N
CAST FLU WASH
D I F S E U
SEVERE SUPERB
R D E E T E
```

83

```
ASH DEW
L U A E
STRANGE
O R G D
LINEN
I C R E
DIAMOND
L N U G
EYE SEE
```

84

```
CLARINET
CENTRAL
TRANCE
CATER
TEAR
ARE
REAR
CARER
CRATER
REACTOR
CREATORS
```

85

```
V E C A B
KANGAROO CORE
N G O C E E
HISS WOOL BEN
S H N S Z
THIEF BUTCHER
L P T H
ANTLERS BOOTS
A S O C O A
FRY STAR LILY
R F E U B K
FOAL COMPOSER
W Y T B Y D
```

86

```
PRIOR PROLONG
E N E E R W Y
PENNANT INNER
P O D G A
ENCRYPT ASSET
R E I M K E
UNDISGUISED
E C M E L S
DREAM RESPECT
I E T T A
TIMER CARTOON
O U S O A N C
REDHEAD WASTE
```

87

```
JEWEL M QUIZ B
A A E EMU OVAL
CLIMATE ALSO S
K S S TAR A PIG
POTATO R FALSE
O N CITY E A N
TANGLE A ORANGE
G E ALLOW B E
GOBLIN O NOODLE
A A D KNEE U
TASTE A ROTTEN
ELK A RUN X E
T FLEA ECLIPSE
HERE TAX I E
R EDGE T PLEAT
```

88

```
BRICK
R R
U E A
SALAD
H A D
A E
UNDER
```

89

```
   T U B S
S W A N   O P E N
I   T I N   A
S C A R   N E W T
E   U   E   E
    F E A T H E R
  F   N     D
B L I S T E R
U   A   M
S T U D   A W A Y
T   D I M   R
P E E L   E A S Y
R   E   L   H
```

94

```
F R O S T
U   U   T
N U T   P
N O S E Y
Y   I D L O
G R E E N
```

95

```
    S A D
   D A S H
  S H A D E
 S H A R E D
C R A S H E D
S E A R C H E D
```

100

```
C O M I C   P I L O T
U   E   H   E   A   A
B U S   A I D   W I N G
E   S   L   A     G
  M A S K   L A B E L
E   G       A     E
S C E N T   W E L L
C   A   I     L   P
A R M   M E T   O I L A
P   U   I   C     O A
E N D E D   H O N E Y
```

90

```
  E A T
 G A T E
G R E A T
G R A T E D
T R A G E D Y
G O T R E A D Y
```

96

```
S P I C E   V O L T A G E
T   M   P   I   O   R   N
I M P R O V E   G A M M A
C   E   C   I       M
K E T C H U P   C H A F E
Y   U       A   T   L
  H O S P I T A L I T Y
T   U   A       E   B
R E S I T   A M M O N I A
O   I   T       T   N
P L A C E   U N T R I E D
I   I   R   S     V   I
C A D E N C E   S W E A T
```

91

```
  D   T   B   B   C   W
M E T E O R   R E H E A T
L   A   U   A   E   I
B E A M   T A N   F A T E
T   A   D   E       T
P E N C I L   Y O G U R T
    A           A
E V E N U P   R E S T E D
E   A       U       N
S N U G   T U B   T R O D
D   L   E   B   R   U
S O L E M N   E N E R G Y
R   E   T   R   E   H
```

97

```
D O L L   L
M A T C H
W I N D O W
S A D D L E S
  S P H I N X
  S K U N K
  K I W I
```

The magician's name is
DANDINI

101

```
  F   W       B
T I G E R S   I
  R   T O W E R
K E Y   S A N D
  S   M E N D S
```

102

1 Scare
2 Canoe
3 Dance
4 Snake.
The material is a **ROCK**.

92

Abandoned, Orchestra, Strongest,
Delivered, Desperate, Interrupt.
The city is **DENVER.**

98

Plastic, Freedom, Manager, Another,
Weather, Grilled, Mineral.
The city is **SEATTLE.**

103

```
  T   U     M   F
P R O M   U G L Y
A   P O P   O
K I W I   P U R R
N   R   E   I
    D E N T I S T
  C     A     T
F L I P P E R
E   I   B
P A I R   G A L E
N   A S H   E
B E L T   T E A M
R   E   H   T
```

104

1 Still 2 Laugh 3 Head 4 Dice
5 Exam 6 Medals 7 Salad 8 Duet
9 Tail.
Ghosts swim in **THE DEAD SEA**!

93

```
T R A V E L S   G R A B
I   N   L   O   O   U
D E N I M   C   A W A Y
E     D   S K I D S
  D E C K S   A     P
F L E A   U   S M I L E
A   F   N   O   C   G
R A R E   K E N N E L S
```

99

```
T A B L E
R   A
A   L   S
I N L E T
N   O   E
    O   P
B O N E S
```

105

	LIS	TEN
DAM	PED	ANT
MED	LAR	

106

The captain is the skipper of
a **TRAWLER**

107

108

109

1 Panda
2 Bench
3 Money
4 Teddy.
The adjective is **ANNOYED**.

110

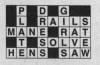

111

1 Basin 2 Money 3 Broom
4 Horse 5 Child 6 Bunny
7 Fight.

The activity is **SNORING**!

112

113

114

BALL, BILL, SILL, SILK, SINK,
LINK, LINE

115

The boy is trying to catch
SHRIMPS.

116

117

1 Jelly
2 Honey
3 Today
4 Milky.
The boat has a **LEAK.**

118

119

1 Croak 2 Short 3 Pilot 4 Carol
5 Snake.
The girl's name is **CHLOE.**

120

121

MAIN, LAIN, LOIN, LOON, LOOM,
DOOM, DOOR.

122

1 Green 2 Train 3 Fever 4 Baker.
The type of dog is a **RETRIEVER.**

123

124

125

1 Swarm 2 Buggy 3 Alien 4 Roses.
The word is **SMUGGLERS**.

130

1 Core
2 Care
3 Hare
4 Hard
5 Herd.

134

The weather forecast is for
DRIZZLE

126

The boy is waiting for his
PUDDING

131

135

127

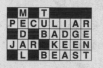

128

1 Unties
2 Unite
3 Tune
4 Net
5 Tone
6 Notes
7 Stoned.

STUNNED is the adjective.

132

```
J O K E R   E   B A N G   B
A   N   A   C O O     E X A M
C H E E T A H   T I L L   K
K   E   I   O A T   I   B E D
D O L L O P   O   T H E R E
A   E   I T E M   R A N
W A D D L E   Q   S E C R E T
  S   G   C R U S H   R   R
C H E E S E   A   A N I M A L
U   X   A   C L I P S   A
F R I L L   A   E M P L O Y
F A T   A   N I T   A E   E
  Z   I D E A   U N C O V E R
J O I N   R I B   A   E   E
R   N O S Y   A   W O R L D
```

136

The girl wants to take home
a **HAMSTER**

133

```
    C Z   A N T   C D
F O R E S T   A F R A I D
    W   R   H     B A   S
H A L O   E E L   B O N E
    R     N E       E
A D D E R S   T A B B Y
    G           I
    B E G I N   G A G G L E
    O     O A     A
E D A M   O L D   D O D O
I   A   D   G E D
K E N N E L   E A S T E R
S   E   E A T   K   R
```

137

1 Bear 2 Reindeer 3 Tiger 4 Camel
5 Bat 6 Mole 7 Horse: **ANIMALS**

129

1 Palace
2 Turtle
3 Middle
4 Damage
5 Couple
6 Decade.

The joke is : What do you
call a snowman in summer?
A **PUDDLE**!

138

1 Geese 2 Cygnet 3 Wide 4 Crown
5 Sofa 6 Winter 7 Tennis 8 French
9 Small: **END OF TERM**.

139

```
  P   A   T   S       J   F
P A S S P O R T       A W A Y
R       T   R   E     R   M
S C A R   C I T Y     B O Y
E       O   H   S     A   U
B L I N D   C O M P A S S
      A   D   N     O
J A N U A R Y   B L A C K
  M   T   A   O     O   E
D A Y   O W L S   G A L E
  Z   P   I   C   I   Z
R O M E N   A   R   Y
  N   N   G   R   E
```

140

```
B L A D E   S   E V I L   P
A   L   V   O F F   I R O N
G A L L E R Y   F A D E   L
G   O   R   A X E   O   O A T
A L W A Y S   C   Z E B R A
G   C   C O A T   E   O K
E D I T O R   G   S N E E Z E
  I   O   A R E N A   J   I
E N T R A P   N   B R E A T H
V   A   T   S T A R   C   A
E Q U A L   Q   E S T E E M
N U T   A   U S E   T L S
  E   I S L E   A C R O B A T
W E L L   A R C   A   O   E
  N   L I C K   H   P O W E R
```

141

```
B I G     B A M B I
E   L     E   I     C
A V A L A N C H E
C   D     R   R     E
H A I L   N O A H
    A   M   W   A
A S T R O N A U T
R     O   T   V   E
M A R C H   E N D
```

142

```
G A T E S
I   U   R
F   R   S
T O K E N
S   E   A
    Y   I
E A S E L
```

143

```
  S   H   I   C C T
P A R E N T   H E L M E T
  I   R   A P E   A   N
B L U E   L   A   W A N D
  O       Y A P   P   I
F R E S H   P   B E A S T
  Y   M A P L E   R
C H E S S   L   G R E E N
  A     W E B     E
E G G S   A   B O Y S
  R   O   F I N   A   O
M I N U T E   J O K E R S
  D   P   R   O   E   E
```

144

```
P E A R L   B   S L O W   S
A   T   I   A L L   H A T E
D E L I V E R   E C H O   O
L   A   I   K I D   E   M O P
O N S I D E   G   D W E L L
C   M   V O T E   G   N   A
K A R A T E   R   S E Q U I N
A   G   N E I G H   U   C
D E T E C T   B   O P E N E R
A   E   O   T E A R   I   S
T O X I C   W   E N T R A P
E A T   O   E L F   I   O   I
S   J A I L   A N N O Y E D
S I Z E   V A N   T   A   L
S   T A K E   G   H I L L Y
```

145

1 A 2 At 3 Sat 4 Last 5 Stale
6 Castle 7 Satchel

146

1 Sunday 2 Skin 3 Snake 4 Shuts
5 Scare A Black B Bones C Boat
D Beard E Bored: **SKATEBOARD**

147

```
    C   L   M U G   T   C
B A N A N A   A L W A Y S
    C   M   G G I C
S T A B   P I G   G A L E
    U       I L       E
E S C A P E   E X A M S
        N         X
  P E T A L   S L E D G E
    A       A E       E
I R O N   U S E   F A N G
    E   O G S I T
S N A T C H   A R N O L D
    T   E   S A W   S E
```

148

```
F A N   D I D   Q U A R R E L
R   I   R   U   U D A O
E X P L A I N   A I M   I V Y
E       M G C I L       A
Z E B R A   A R K   T O W E L
E   A       R       A T
R O T O R   E B B   S H Y L Y
    U   E E O
B A C O N   S E A   B A R O N
E   O       U       A A
L I M I T   J E T   E I G H T
O   P   H E I X       U
V I A   E E L   F L I P P E R
E   S   I   L U S E A
D E S T R O Y   L O T   A L L
```

149

```
    B   E   D   H F K
G A N D E R   O L I V E R
  T   E   I L L   L   N
A M E N   L   L   M A N E
  A       L A Y       E
S N A C K   T   B I B L E
    G   I G L O O   A
S P E N D   A   G A T E S
  A       U S A       I
C R A B   D     H U G E
  R   I   D O E A   H
B O T T L E   N I N E T Y
  T   E   R   T D Y
```

150

1 Crush
2 Dress
3 Trunk
4 Quiet.
Conkers grow on a
CHESTNUT tree.

151

```
Y A H O O
E   O   L
A   L   S
S W I S H
T   D   E
    A   L
R O Y A L
```

152

1 Moo 2 Meow 3 Gobble 4 Roar
5 Tweet 6 Howl 7 Cluck 8 Quack
9 Bark 10 Grunt: **GIANT PANDA**

153

```
    F   J   S       B
HULA    HOUR
    L   N   Y       L
ALBUM   SLY
    A       C       E
    AIRPORT         T
    F   Y       B
CRY     SWARM
    A   G       E
CITY    BANK
    D   M       S   G
```

154

1 Coat, talk
2 Poor, read
3 Love, even
4 Flea, aunt
5 Beds, seat
6 Menu, ugly
7 Hour, race
8 Hive, evil.

The word is **TREASURE**.

155

```
    B   S   BUS E   F
BOTTLE  CAMERA
    N   E   E   RUE E
SNOW    TIE SAND
    E       L   A   C
    STABLE  MARCH
    A       I
    HOTEL   ELBOWS
    A   E   X   A
AMEN    MAP RAIN
    M   E   O   A   A   T
SEASON  NUGGET
    R   T   SADER
```

156

```
KIOSK   F   HOOD    C
    E   F   N   ACE IDOL
SETBACK ITEM    R
    T   E   V   EGG V   AGE
RUNNER  H   EQUIP
    E   U   UNIT N   I
LENTIL  D   STATIC
    E   T   EJECT C   C
PLAYER  A   ANTHEM
    A   R   X   FLAT O   I
COMMA   A   EARWIG
TRY C   ROD     A   R
    B   ATOM    REPLICA
ZINC    EMU AST
    T   TOUR    GLTE
```

157

```
    B   B   I       B
NEAR    ARO CORE
    A   O   E   BRANCH
SKATE   END
    H   S   C
    CHEETAH
    A   R   E
EMU     BENCH
    E   I   P   A   A
DRUM    LAKE
    A   P   E       E
```

158

1 Pet
2 Pat
3 Sat
4 Say
5 Day.

159

```
ABOVE       CUB
    F   W   Y   A   R
TANGERINE
    E   S   R   A
RAYS    COOK
    N   A   B       F
ORCHESTRA       S
    O   H   E   E   S
NET     START
```

160

```
TABLE
O   E   U
A   A
SOCKS   S
T   H   A   G
    E
PASTE
```

161

```
REEF    JOKE
O   X   L   A   N
PEA ANKLE
E   COW     M
SIT N   SPY
CLIMATE
KEY O   ANT
N   WAR W
EAGLE   TOE
E   U   R   L   E
LAMB    HEAT
```

162

```
B   C   B   S   S   G
FATHER  HOCKEY
    L   I   ARE A   N
CLAP    V   L   RAIN
    E   ELF     U
STALK   I   CHESS
    C   IGLOO   G
SPEND   A   DIGIT
    A   ACT     C
CLAW    D   H   DRIP
    A   OUSE    A   C
SCHOOL  FAMILY
    E   L   T   T   P   E
```

163

```
JAR CUB ELASTIC
A   U   R   R   N   F   H   A
CABBAGE JET INN
K   Z   A   O   E   N   T
DAISY   KEY RANGE
A   L   F       E   E
WALTZ   AXE HERON
    O   S   A   A
RODEO   TAR SAVED
E   W       T   A   E
QUIET   ASH CANAL
U   N   E   P   L   R   I
END MAP ICEBERG
S   L   P   L   N   A   A   H
THEATRE GEM ROT
```

164

```
TREE
DIVER
    DICE
PUDDING
MALLET
    HIVES
    ARMS
```

The kitten's name is **TIDDLES**

165

```
HARE    CHEF
O   A   B   O   A
SKI RAPID
E   L   IE      E
SAW A   DAD
    CACKLES
STY F   SHY
A       APE A
NEWTS   RAW
T   E   T   T   N
ANTS    ASKS
```

166

1 Water
2 Igloo
3 Zebra
4 Adult
5 Right
6 Dirty.

The Quizkids are going to
see a **WIZARD**.

167

```
  B  B  C  B  H  B
S L E I G H   E D I T O R
  E   R   A I R   S   N
B A L D   L   R   S A N G
  T   K E Y       E
O S C A R   A   F I F T Y
  A   A P R I L   E
S C R A M   L   Y A W N S
  A   G Y M     U
A M E N   U   A   B A R K
  E   A   A R M U S
T R E M O R   B O D I E S
  A   E D A S S
```

168

The boy is running from a
JELLYFISH

169

The boy has got **MEASLES**

170

```
  B  I  C  A  S  K
S U M M E R   R A C H E L
  L   P   A I R   A N
P L U S   W O   B A N K
  E     L O W     E
A T L A S   Z   G I R L S
    E   A B O V E   A
B L O O D   N   M A G I C
  E     F E D     R
S T E M   I   U   C H O P
  T   A   G U M   A N
S E A R C H   B A L L E T
  R   E T O F D
```

171

```
R A C E     W E E D
A   A     C   W   A   N
V E T   O C E A N   C
E     F I N   S   C
N I L   S   A G E
    L A N T E R N
A L P   A   M U D
D     B I B   O
D R I L L   A N D
E     C   E   N   G
R E E D   I D L E
```

172

The woman is an **ACTRESS**

173

1 Stare 2 Grape 3 Drive
4 Clone: **PRUNE**

174

```
D R A F T   S   T
E   B   I V O R Y
E   L A P   L   P
D R E W   M O V E
  O   L I E   A
S E A S   R A T S
  O   C   P E G A
C A R V E   E   L
  K   E   N U D G E
```

175

```
  B  O  A  A  G  E
H O P P E D   H O N E S T
  R   E   D O E   A   C
L I O N   E   A   T E A M
  N     R E D     P
I G L O O   R   A L I E N
    I   A D U L T   C
S P E A R   P   E N E M Y
  A     S T Y     I
C R A B   A   A   B O N E
  C   E   V A N   A U
D E C A D E   K A R A T E
  L   K S S E E
```

176

```
K A Y A K ■ F ■ J A I L ■ O
E ■ E ■ N ■ A G O ■ I N C H
S E A S I C K ■ S L A P ■ E
T ■ S ■ F ■ E A T ■ B ■ F A T
R O T T E R ■ ■ L ■ O Z O N E
E ■ H ■ H O P E ■ V ■ O ■ A
L U X U R Y ■ A ■ L E A D E R
■ S ■ M ■ M A N G O ■ D ■ R
P E B B L E ■ D ■ C A M E R A
A ■ O ■ E ■ D A T A ■ I ■ P
G E N I E ■ E ■ ■ L E T T E R
E V E ■ C ■ E N D ■ Q ■ I ■ I
■ E ■ S H I P ■ A Q U A T I C
G N A T ■ ■ E L F ■ I ■ L ■ O
■ T ■ Y A W N ■ T ■ P L E A T
```